Praise for
TALES FROM SCHWARTZGARTEN

For Christopher John d'Argaville Wood

ORCHARD BOOKS
338 Euston Road, London NW1 3BH
Orchard Books Australia
Level 17/207 Kent Street, Sydney, NSW 2000

ISBN 978 1 40833 181 1

First published in Great Britain in 2014
Text © Christopher William Hill 2014

A CIP catalogue record for this book is available from the British
Library.

10 9 8 7 6 5 4 3 2 1 (hardback)

Printed in Great Britain

Orchard Books is a division of Hachette Children's Books, an
Hachette UK company.

www.hachette.co.uk

Schwartzgarten map illustration by Artful Doodlers © Orchard Books 2013
Guidebook illustrations © Chris Naylor 2014

TALES FROM SCHWARTZGARTEN

THE LILY-LIVERED PRINCE

Christopher William Hill

ORCHARD

THE CITY OF SCHWARTZGARTEN

OLD TOWN

9. Library
10. Park – to Walk Children or Execute Prisoners
11. Home of the Locksmith's Boy

18. Emeté Talbor's Menagerie
19. Schwartzgarten Museum
20. Bildstein and Bildstein
21. House of Old Engelfried

22. The Old Chop House
23. Schwartzgarten Opera House
24. Old Schwartzgarten Cemetery
25. Main Gate to the Great City

A Word of Warning to Weak-minded Children

This short history of Prince Eugene was set down on paper more than twenty years ago. In that time, the book has been widely read. While most scholars with brains in their heads approve of the story I have attempted to tell, others have doubted my wisdom in relating to children a tale so dark as to put the hairs upright on their scalps. And to that I say 'Pah!' War is a messy business – and a large part of this book is taken up with war, as is the way in all history books. Swords are drawn and heads come off. There is blood and there is gore and that is all there is to say on the subject.

If you are firm of stomach and sound of mind, then continue, reader. If not, then return to your stamp collection or spinning top, or whatever other idle pursuit fills your sorry days. You are not the child to read my book, so be gone back to your dark corner.

From the pen of Kristifan Von Hoffmeyer,
Historian of the City of Schwartzgarten
and Keeper of the Northern Manuscripts

DESCENDANTS *of the*
SCHWARTZGARTEN

DESPINA OF LÜCHMÜNSTER — *m. Siegfried the Sane*

ALBERTO *m. Aurelia*   **RUFUS**   **DMITRI** *(The Archduke)*

EUGENE — *m. Euphenia*

WILHELM *(line dies out)*

IMPERIAL FAMILY

VLADISLAS THE BRUTAL — *m. Irina The Fair*

VOLKOFF

MAXIMILIAN
(poisoned at birth)

The Founding
of the City of
Schwartzgarten

———◆◆◆———

I N THE depths of a cruel winter, seven families from distant lands journeyed across a strange and barren terrain. To the north there were mountains and to the south an impenetrable forest, made perilous by the presence of wolves and bears. Weary from travelling, they settled down to rest beside a river that coiled like a vast, black serpent through the icy wasteland.

The river had frozen deep so they could not catch fish. The earth was hard as flint, so they could not dig for food.

'We must eat,' said a man, whose name was Offenbach. 'Our stomachs cry out for food, and if we do not answer that call then we shall surely die.'

The Hungry Seven, for that is how History has named the travellers, were desperate indeed. It seemed that Fate had forsaken the Seven. Cast out into the wilderness, they hoped for Life but prepared for Death.

Fate, however, is a sly master, and was not prepared to see the Hungry Seven die for want of food and warmth. As life ebbed away from the starving travellers the sky turned black with Ravens, obscuring the pale winter sun with the beating of their wings. The Ravens spiralled down around the Seven, bearing scraps of food, though the travellers knew not from where. The Hungry Seven felt the cold, hard beaks against their cracked lips, and they were thankful. The Ravens sheltered them with their feathers and again, the Hungry Seven were thankful.

So it was that the Seven survived that bitter winter. They survived and what is more, they prospered. As spring gave life to the land, they built simple timber buildings on the banks of the dark river. In time, the timber shacks gave way to buildings of stone and slate. As the City slowly grew, the descendants of the Hungry Seven grew ever hungrier. Though their bellies were full, they were hungry for wealth and hungry for power. And all that they wanted was theirs to have, the Ravens saw to that: the birds were protectors of the City and Guardians of the Seven. In return they sought nothing but an offering of rye bread and river water once a year at the Festival of the Departed Souls.

The names of six families of the Seven are known to all true-born citizens of Schwartzgarten: the names of Offenbach, Koski, Engelfried, Dressler, Talbor and Van Veenen. They were Illustrious and Wise and Strong. Their names were carved in tablets of slate that their Great Fame might live on through the generations.

But Legend does not record the name of the Seventh family. It was a cursed name that was struck from the annals of the City many centuries ago. At the head of this family was a man whom Fate had marked out for blacker deeds. His eyes were as dark as the cunning wolf and his heart was cold as granite.

'The Ravens demand too much of us,' said the one whose name is unknown. 'Our rye bread and our river water is ours to do with as we please.'

The Founding Families were in fear of the man, and bowed to his wishes, though their hearts were troubled.

When, on the Eve of the Festival of the Departed

Souls, the Ravens gathered to claim that which was rightfully theirs to claim, there was neither bread to eat nor water to drink. The Ravens cried a curse on the Seventh Family, which the one whose name is unknown repaid by killing seven of the birds with blade and shot and fire. It was a Dark Act indeed and the curse grew sevenfold to engulf all of the Founding Families.

The one who committed the Dark Act was cast out for his evil by the elders of each Family, banished beyond the City walls and condemned to wander in shame throughout the ages. But it was not enough to undo the curse. The Ravens were protectors no more, but scavengers that spread fear and disease. Plague came and bloodshed followed. And down and down through the centuries came darkness and terror unimaginable.

The curse today has long passed, undone by the crawling passage of the years and the certain knowledge that the name of the Seventh Family is now unknowable. But what is equally certain to those that believe in such things, and is indeed recorded in the Northern Manuscripts, is this: when the Seventh of the Seven Families returns to Schwartzgarten, the Darkest of Dark Days will come once more to the Great City.

As related and translated by Grigorius Von Hoffmeyer,
Historian of the City of Schwartzgarten
and Keeper of the Northern Manuscripts
(deceased)

THE LOCKSMITH'S BOY

T HE STORY of the founding of the city of Schwartzgarten at the beginning of this book was translated by my late father, long cold in his grave, who was keeper of the Northern Manuscripts before me.

For those who are not familiar with the ancient city of Schwartzgarten, the name is derived from the old Northern languages – that is to say 'Schwartz' meaning black and 'Garten' meaning garden.

The word black, of course, refers to the colour of the serpent-like river as it flows darkly through our great city. But the word garden is misleading here – as nothing flourished on the banks of the river. I can only imagine it was meant as a joke, though it is by no means amusing to me.

It is quite true that the name of one of the Seven Founding Families is no longer known to living man. It is an ancient name of a thousand years ago or more and has been lost to the sands of time.

Each in their turn, the remaining Six of the Seven Founding Families ruled over Schwartzgarten. Some were good and just, others were cruel and greedy – but of all the Six, no family was more greedy for power than the House of Talbor.

At the time our story begins, some seventy-five years ago, Schwartzgarten was ruled over by the tyrant Emeté Talbor, who had seized power nineteen years earlier. Talbor modelled himself after Emperor Xavier, who had ruled over Schwartzgarten three hundred years before. Even his clothes had been made to resemble those of the Emperor.

Talbor did not believe in the modern world – in steam trains, or factories, or even clockwork. As far as he was concerned, the sun revolved around the earth and he himself was at the very centre of the universe. And in his reign of terror, he did all that he could to keep the clock from moving on.

As a child he had wanted to do unpleasant things to people, and often did.

'It is important to study your enemy closely,' Talbor's father had cautioned his son, presenting him with a sword made by the city's master goldsmiths, to mark the infant's fifth birthday.

And Talbor had taken these words to heart, as he

polished his sword carefully. It was the very same sword, in fact, that he used to slay his father on the occasion of his seventh birthday.

Emeté Talbor grew up craving power. When he was of age, he took for his bride the daughter of the House of Van Veenen, one of the richest families of the Hungry Seven, and his power grew. He served as a general in Crown Prince Alberto's army, and used his wealth and influence to lead a revolt against the Prince. In three bloody battles outside the city walls, Talbor and his troops fought with the Imperial Army, who were still loyal to Alberto. But though the Crown Prince was a brave soldier, his army was not strong enough to defeat Talbor. The Imperial Family were driven from Schwartzgarten and fled to the north, where they made their home in the Summer Palace.

A fact should be noted here – Crown Prince Alberto was one of three brothers. Beside his youngest brother, Archduke Dmitri, Alberto had an identical twin, Rufus, born minutes later than the Crown Prince himself. Mark this well, for it will be important to my tale.

Talbor was victorious and settled in the palace in the heart of the great city. Though his wife was blessed with fifteen children, not a single child lived beyond its first birthday, Talbor saw to that; so terrified was he that they would one day grow to challenge his power. And though he loved his wife better than his golden sword, he grew fearful of her too – and to prove his love, he kept her nose on a gold chain around his neck, threaded beside those of his mother and father. And he swore to wear her nose from the day he cut off her head to the day he might himself die.

By law, copies of Talbor's portrait hung in every house, shop and office across the city. And, in one such house, in a cramped alleyway close to the Street of the Seven Locksmiths, lived one of the heroes of my tale.

The boy, for he had no name as such at this time, was known to all as the Locksmith's Boy – though he did not work as a locksmith himself. He worked, instead, as a pot boy in the great house of Old Engelfried, one of the descendants of the Hungry Seven. The boy, in his thirteenth year, was unremarkable to look at – shorter than many and thinner than many more. He had chestnut hair, and legs and arms as would be expected in a boy of his age. And that is all that needs to be said, except that his hands were as cold as marble.

Old Engelfried was a kind master and had a favourite son, named Alesander, three years older than the Locksmith's Boy and half a head taller. He had dark hair and an open face and was kinder still than his father. Often he would talk to the boy if he passed him in the street or on the stair.

The Locksmith's Boy's bedroom was at the top of a small house, pushed so close against the roof that he had to crawl into bed at night. And, as the house slept, with the wick of his candle trimmed low, he would take out a bag of lead soldiers that he kept hidden behind a loose stone in the wall and line them up in neat rows. He could name every regiment of Prince Alberto's army, every general and every banner ever raised in battle.

'I will be a great hero, Mother,' said the Locksmith's Boy one evening as he stared up at the framed print of Emeté Talbor that hung from the wall. 'I will serve in battle and I will cut down hundreds of enemy soldiers. I will defeat Emeté Talbor and Prince Alberto will return home to Schwartzgarten.'

His mother smacked him hard around the ears. 'You'll never mount up to more than a heap of curselings,' she chided. 'Hero indeed! Your father would be turning in his grave. If he was dead. Which he isn't, more's the pity.' She bustled around the kitchen, carrying food from the stove to the table. 'Emeté Talbor is a gracious tyrant and bounteous in his mercies,' she continued. 'You'd do well to remember that.'

'But, Mother—' protested the Locksmith's Boy.

The woman waved her hands to silence her son and pushed her ear against the wall. 'I know he's there,' she croaked, listening out for any murmur of sound from their landlord, who lived in the house next door. 'Writing down my every word. Every precious thought in my head. Always looking for ways to report me to the Vigils and get me hanged.'

You may of course be asking, 'And who were the Vigils? And what part do they play in this story?' To which I answer, be patient, and read my words in the order I have laid them out for you.

The Locksmith's Boy's mother slammed a bowl of food on the table and her son wrinkled up his nose in disgust.

'Bacon and potatoes again,' he groaned with a shake of his head. 'Why is it bacon and potatoes every night?'

'You'll eat it up and you'll be thankful,' snapped the woman.

'I'm sick of the sight of bacon and potatoes,' said the Locksmith's Boy. 'Father hates it as well.'

'Your father's beyond help,' said the boy's mother, opening a cupboard door and taking out a dry loaf of bread and a pot of rancid butter.

'And dry bread,' moaned the boy. 'I bet Emeté Talbor doesn't eat like this. He has the best of everything and we have the bread and scrapings.'

'My own son a traitor!' wailed the woman. 'We're done for! Done for!' An icy breeze whipped around the kitchen and she broke the bread, which shattered into a dozen pieces. She attempted to glue the loaf back together with the sour butter, all the time muttering, 'Pay homage to the tyrant! Be grateful for your lot in this life!'

But the Locksmith's Boy shook his head again. 'I'm not going to pay homage,' he said. 'I don't have anything to be grateful for.'

At this the woman glowered at her son. 'You should be grateful to him for keeping your neck on your shoulders, that's what you should be grateful for.'

After supper the Locksmith's Boy was sent to fetch his drunkard father home from the Old Chop House, at the very heart of the great city. Tobacco smoke hung about the tavern like a thick curtain and it was impossible to see more than two paces in any direction. Waiters forced their way through the heaving room, carrying plates heaped with veal steaks and pickled cabbage. The Locksmith's Boy groped blindly through the fog of smoke, clutching at tables to steady himself on his way. At the very end of the bar sat the boy's father, a small man with skin as brown as a walnut shell. As is right and proper for the father of a Locksmith's Boy, the man was a locksmith. Or rather, the man *had* been a locksmith, but rye beer had set his hands to trembling. It had also loosened his tongue. As the Locksmith's Boy pushed on through the crowded room his father was holding court to anyone who would listen, all the time eating sweet dill pickles from a jar.

'I'll tell you another thing about that swine Talbor,' he slurred, pulling a drinking companion towards him by the scruff of the neck. 'That menagerie he keeps, with all those animals – you know what they're for? Well, I'll *tell* you.' He stopped to dip his hand into the jar, pulling out another pickle. 'He throws his enemies into that menagerie to be eaten alive. *Alive*, I say. The lion...and the...and the rhinoceros. And all the other animals besides. I heard it from a...from a very *reliable* source, between you and me.' He attempted to tap his nose conspiratorially with his finger but slipped and stuck the pickle in his eye. 'He's a madman, sure enough,' he continued, rubbing his eye and crunching the pickle. 'And I'll tell you *this* for nothing—'

'Come on home, Father,' said the Locksmith's Boy quickly, 'before you land us all in jail for treason.'

It was one thing to complain about Emeté Talbor at home, but quite another to do so in a busy tavern where the Vigils might overhear.

What is that you say? I have *still* not told you of the Vigils? To which I now say, 'The patient reader will be rewarded in good time, and I will thank you not to interrupt again.'

The Locksmith slipped on the pools of rye beer as his son attempted to lead him towards the door and out into the street, where they were embraced by a damp mist that drifted in from the river.

'Talbor's got a giraffe too!' whispered the Locksmith.

'That's right, Father,' said the boy.

'And hippos!' laughed the Locksmith. 'Not one, mind you...*two* hippos. Hippos have pink milk!'

'Yes, Father,' said the boy.

'Ah,' said the Locksmith and shook his head. 'I've told you that story before.'

As they weaved their way along the cobbles the Locksmith leant against the wall and retched into the gutter.

'That's better,' he gurgled. 'Now hold me steady, boy.'

The Locksmith's Boy held his father firmly by the shoulders, steering him safely through the narrow streets towards home. From time to time the man would stumble on a loose cobblestone, all the while swinging his fists as he fought imaginary rhinos and hippos, but at last the boy successfully hauled his father into bed (or rather a straw mattress beside the kitchen stove), where the man lay on his back, snoring and snorting like a wild beast from Emeté Talbor's menagerie.

'One day,' thought the Locksmith's Boy as he heaved off his father's boots, 'one day I'll leave Schwartzgarten far behind me. I'll set out for battle and return a hero.'

Perhaps this was the case and perhaps it was not. But if you do not read on I can tell you no more.

EMETÉ TALBOR

THE DAY of Alesander Engelfried's sixteenth birthday dawned clear and bright. But there was a chill in the air that gnawed at the bones. In the kitchens of Old Engelfried's house, preparations were underway for the birthday banquet. Pastries were baked, jellies were set in copper moulds and meat was slowly roasted over the open fire. In the cold room, ornate sculptures were carved from solid blocks of ice, resembling fantastical creatures from books of myth and fable.

All day long the Locksmith's Boy ran errands, scrubbed floors and plucked birds ready to cook on the spit. At midday he was sent to the forest to collect cloudberries for a mousse, to crown the banquet table.

The trees towered so tightly together in the part of the forest where the berries grew thickest that they obliterated the sky above. As the boy made his way into a clearing, he discovered a raven at his feet. The creature was lying motionless, illuminated by a single shard of golden sunlight that pierced the high branches, and the boy eyed it hungrily.

'After all,' he thought, 'raven will undoubtedly make a more interesting meal than bacon and potatoes.'

'But maybe you're not dead at all,' he said, picking up the bird and cradling it in his hands. 'Have you fallen from your nest?' he whispered.

As the boy gently prodded the bird, one of the creature's eyes rolled out into the palm of his hand.

Suddenly a voice cried, 'Step away!'

The Locksmith's Boy looked up to see two foot soldiers approaching through the bracken. One soldier was tall and the other was short, but both were rolling drunk from beetroot schnapps.

'To catch and kill a raven is a privilege of the tyrant Talbor alone!' shouted the short soldier.

'I didn't kill it,' stammered the Locksmith's Boy. 'It was already dead.'

'What is your name?' demanded the tall soldier.

But the Locksmith's Boy could not reply. It seemed that his head had been emptied of all thought.

And as he stood mutely, there was a rustling between the trees. A figure of a man on horseback appeared and the soldiers gasped and took a step backwards. Though the man was not large, he was solidly built and rose up on the saddle like a creature from the boy's darkest nightmares. He had piercing black eyes that sparkled like nuggets of polished jet and a long, untidy mane of dark hair. There were golden rings on every finger and round his neck he wore a raven wing in a silver mount and three dried and shrivelled noses, threaded on a golden chain.

Two immense dogs with silver collars studded with iron spikes bounded behind him.

'Come, Hubris! Come, Nemesis!' cried the man as he drove his horse forward.

Scrabbling over the black dirt of the forest floor came a third dog, a yapping pug that twitched so quickly and so violently at the neck that it seemed it might have three heads rather than the usual one. This dog, as history records, was known as Cerberus.

The man, I need not tell you, clever reader, was Emeté Talbor.

'Who is this?' demanded Talbor as his horse whinnied and came to a halt.

'Raven killer, sir,' said the tall soldier, attempting to stay sober and upright.

Though the Locksmith's Boy had gazed at his mother's framed print of Talbor since his earliest days, nothing had prepared him for meeting the man in the flesh.

Talbor leant down from the saddle and picked up the raven by its fractured wing. 'You know what we do with raven killers?' he growled, staring so fiercely that the Locksmith's Boy imagined himself skewered by the tyrant's gaze. Talbor tossed the raven into the deep undergrowth and Cerberus ran yapping into the bracken to feast on the dead bird. 'Take him back to the city. We will make an example of the boy.'

With a click of his spurs he galloped off through the trees, followed closely by the whining hounds. As Emeté Talbor was swallowed up by the darkness of the forest, ravens rose in alarm from the branches of the trees.

'Look out!' cried the tall soldier, holding his hands to his face as the birds flapped desperately about them.

The short soldier stepped backwards, falling heavily against a wolf trap, hidden by hunters beneath a scattering of leaves. There was a crisp snap of metal jaws.

'Well, help me then!' cried the soldier. 'My tunic's caught!'

As the tall soldier crouched down to free his comrade from the wolf trap, the Locksmith's Boy seized his moment. He turned on his heel and ran.

'Wait!' screamed the tall soldier. 'Stop!'

But the boy had no intention of waiting and certainly no desire to stop. He fled from the forest, running back along the path towards the city and the house of the Engelfrieds, where he hid in the busy kitchen.

He spoke not a word of his encounter with Talbor – but it would have been better that he had, for Engelfried believed that Talbor was hunting away from Schwartzgarten and did not know that the tyrant had returned.

It is later that same night that we first meet the Vigils. If you have never learnt of the Vigils and never wish to learn of them, then you might be the better for it. But if you choose to read on, then who am I to stop you?

There had first been Vigils in Schwartzgarten during the reign of Emperor Xavier – indeed, they once served as private guard to that ruler. But the custom had died out, until eighteen years before this tale begins.

In the time of which I write the Vigils were made up of a hundred men, drawn from the richest families in Schwartzgarten. When the eldest son reached the age of sixteen, he was claimed by the Vigils to serve in Emeté Talbor's own private guard. By controlling the first sons, he could control the city.

The Vigils were distinguished by the uncommonness of their uniform. They wore black leather gauntlets and black hooded capes, and about their faces they wore the raven masks that struck fear into the citizens of Schwartzgarten – with hooked beaks and plumage of black raven feathers.

As Alesander was now of age, and as he was the eldest son of Old Engelfried, he was also due to be taken by the Vigils. But Old Engelfried did not want to see his best-beloved son lost to the Vigils. He had arranged that on the eve of Alesander's sixteenth birthday, he would be smuggled from the city to live with a distant cousin on the shores of Lake Taneva. Alas, this was not to be.

Old Engelfried was loyal to Prince Alberto, and had long sought to overthrow the tyrant. His words had found their way back to Emeté Talbor, who was displeased.

It was bitterly cold and the Vigils gathered at the northern corner of Edvardplatz as the great Schwartzgarten bell struck the hour of eight from the Emperor Xavier clock tower. They turned their cloaks against the icy wind.

The Commander of the Guard, whose name was Glattburg, gazed grimly at his men. He was a squat man of middle years, with a closely-cropped head of hair, and a long, thin battle scar stretching from his cheek to his chin. His left eye was carved from marble and his nose, sliced off by Talbor in a fit of anger, had been replaced by a cap of polished silver.

'It's too cold for this,' said a young man from the house of Koski. 'We'd be better off in the Old Chop House drinking, not standing out here.'

'You'll do as I tell you, miserable gutter rats,' spat Glattburg, wiping his marble eye on his tunic and returning it to its socket. 'Now, prepare.'

The Vigils pulled on their gauntlets and lowered their raven masks, melting into the shadows as they observed the descendants of the Hungry Seven processing through the streets of the city, on their way to mark the birthday of Alesander Engelfried. The Van Veenen family led the way, then came the Dresslers and the Offenbachs. The Koski and Engelfried families followed behind. There were no Talbors in the procession - Emeté had slaughtered so many members of his own family that he was the last of the line.

The Locksmith's Boy, who was to serve at table, was already in the large hall of the House of Engelfried when the families assembled. Musicians played, dogs scampered about the floor and Alesander was presented with gifts. The food was wondrous to behold, with roasted meats and pies, and jellies so tall that they seemed to defy the natural law of gravity. Most delicious to the Locksmith's Boy was a small pastry known in Schwartzgarten as an *eagle*, stuffed with chocolate and marzipan. Alesander made certain that his friend had handfuls of the pastries to fill his pockets.

Old Engelfried held up his glass of beetroot schnapps. Outside, the sky had turned a dark and ominous shade of purple.

'A toast to my eldest son, who today has come of age...'

But the words died on his lips. A figure had entered the room, an unbidden guest. The musicians stopped playing and a grave silence descended on the gathering.

'It's the Vigils,' gasped Alesander as Glattburg

stepped forward, searching the crowded room. 'They've come for me.'

'Hide, my boy,' hissed Old Engelfried. 'Don't let them find you. Your cousin will be here soon to take you away to Lake Taneva.'

But it was too late.

'Alesander Engelfried,' cried Glattburg. 'The Vigils have come to claim you!'

'You were not invited,' shouted Old Engelfried. 'Leave this house at once!'

'Be sensible,' said Dressler, who had lost his own favourite son to the Vigils. 'It's hopeless to resist.'

'Not *my* son!' cried Engelfried. 'You can't take him from me!'

In answer, the Vigils gave their raven cry. The cawing was loud enough to drive a man from his senses.

But the worst was still to come. As Engelfried pleaded with the Vigils the door swung open and Emeté Talbor strode in, accompanied by General Akibus, the bravest and most brutal general in Talbor's entire army, known to all as the Dark Count. He was a fat man with a black beard and carried his battle helmet in his hand, adorned with raven feathers.

'Excellency!' exclaimed Engelfried and, as the oldest member of the Hungry Seven, he knelt before Emeté Talbor, as was customary.

'I am here to celebrate the birthday of your son,' said Talbor.

'I...I did not know that you had returned home to Schwartzgarten,' murmured Engelfried.

'And that was why I was not invited?' asked Talbor with a twitching smile.

'Oh, Excellency,' gasped Engelfried.

But Talbor laughed and shook his head. He reached out his hand and pulled Old Engelfried to his feet. 'A gift for your son,' he cried, and waved towards the windows. 'An excellent gift!'

Together with his guests, Engelfried gazed out through the leaded panes of the windows. And as they waited and watched an unexpected sight met their eyes. Two creatures appeared at the far end of Alexis Street below. First came a zebra, galloping fast as a stallion and then a giraffe, running wildly along the cobbles, its neck swaying and its long, grey tongue lolling at the side of its mouth. The Six Families aughed and applauded, though Old Engelfried was uneasy.

The Locksmith's Boy crouched in the darkest corner of the room, not daring to move, hardly daring to breathe.

'The best of all gifts,' laughed Talbor. 'I have set my menagerie free to roam the streets of Schwartzgarten!'

'Thank...you,' stammered Alesander, not certain what best to say.

Old Engelfried turned to Talbor. 'Please,' he whispered. 'I am an old man. Please do not take my son from me.'

'But of course I will take him,' said Talbor, laughing again. 'Alesander is of age.'

The boy cried out, but the Vigils seized him and held him fast. Slowly Glattburg lowered the raven mask over Alesander's face as another Vigil dressed him in his leather gauntlets and hooded cloak.

'No!' gasped the Locksmith's Boy, forgetting himself and stumbling out from the shadows.

'What was that?' spat Talbor. 'Who spoke?' He swung round and glared at the Locksmith's Boy. 'You!' he cried. 'The raven slayer!'

Before Talbor could speak another word, the Locksmith's Boy turned and slipped from the room, running down the wooden staircase and out into the street.

'After the boy!' bawled Glattburg.

Old Engelfried shook his head and moaned in despair as Alesander was dragged from the room. He was defeated.

'Now sit, old man,' cried Talbor. 'Drink. I have brought good wine.'

Old Engelfried sat at the table as Talbor poured him a glass of the wine.

Talbor waved his hand to the Dark Count and the man stepped forward, carrying an ornately carved box. He opened the lid and Talbor lifted out the large glass bottle that was contained within. He held the bottle close to Engelfried's face. Inside sat a black rat, clawing desperately at the glass. The rat was separated by a deep layer of white lily petals from a hunter, a variety of poisonous spider peculiar to the forests of Schwartzgarten, which sat motionless at the very top of the bottle.

'One rat, one spider,' observed Talbor. He shook the bottle gently. 'What do you think will happen?' he asked in an awestruck whisper. 'Will the rat eat the spider or will the spider sting the rat?' He pulled the cork from the bottle and allowed the spider to crawl out onto the back of his black leather gauntlet. '...Or will the spider sting you?'

He held out the spider to Engelfried and the man seemed to age before him. Talbor laughed and returned the spider to the bottle and Engelfried, breathing a sigh of relief, continued to drink. Inside the bottle, the rat burrowed its way through the lily petals, whereupon the hunter stung the rat and the rat consumed the spider and both were dead within moments.

'The Engelfrieds are a revered family among the Seven,' continued Talbor. 'That is why it moved me so greatly to hear of your death.'

Old Engelfried lowered his glass and his eyes widened.

'I know that you have been planning to overthrow me,' said Talbor. 'That it is your wish to restore Prince Alberto to the throne.'

'I told no one,' gasped Engelfried. 'No one but—'

'But me,' said a tall thin man with raven hair and a thin moustache, who emerged slowly from the shadows.

'Volkoff!' cried Engelfried.

As the man Volkoff has now stepped into the scene, it seems the correct time to give him his proper introduction. Volkoff was a cousin of the Imperial Family, and served as

Ambassador to Crown Prince Alberto – and spy to Emeté Talbor. He was trusted by Talbor and he was trusted by Alberto, but neither was right to do so.

'Drink more,' said Talbor. 'This wine is my gift to you, Engelfried.'

Suddenly, Engelfried clutched at his throat.

'As I said,' repeated Talbor as Engelfried crumpled to the floor and spent his last breath, 'I was sorry to hear of your death.' He laughed. 'Now burn the House of Engelfried to the ground.'

⸻⸱⸻

The Locksmith's Boy ran hard along Alexis Street, turning right onto Marshal Podovsky Street, where a lion was terrorising diners in a corner restaurant, and on towards the Street of the Seven Locksmiths. Arriving at the house of his mother and father, he slammed the door shut behind him and bolted it fast.

'What's the matter?' snapped the boy's mother. 'Trying to rattle me into my grave?'

'You have to hide me, Mother!' panted the Locksmith's Boy.

'What have you done?' demanded the woman, jabbing her son in the chest with the tip of her bony finger. 'If you've made trouble for yourself, you can suffer for yourself too. Don't drag me and your father into it.'

'But I was trying to feed us,' protested the boy. 'I found a raven.'

'You can't kill ravens!' cried his mother. 'They'll string you up.'

'I didn't kill it,' groaned the boy. 'It was dead already.'

'Don't even like raven,' said his mother. 'Filthy meat. You've brought shame on the family.'

This was more than the boy could bear.

'And who will drag your father from the tavern at night,' continued his mother, 'if you're locked up and rotting, I ask you that?'

The boy did not have an answer.

Loud voices could be heard in the street outside and dogs howled.

'They're coming for me!' whispered the Locksmith's Boy.

'You'll have us all put to death!' gasped the woman. 'Get out! Get out now, before they hang me as well!'

So the boy fled once more, out through a back door and

across the narrow yard where his mother grew potatoes.

'What's going on?' cried the Landlord, leaning from the window of the next-door house. 'I heard dogs barking.'

The boy did not reply and the Landlord, sensing that the skulking youth was at the root of the trouble, cried out – 'If you're hunting for the Locksmith's Boy, then he's here for the taking!'

Vaulting the low wall beyond the yard the boy turned right into a tight alleyway that ran behind the Street of the Seven Locksmiths. 'I will run to the Old Chop House,' he thought. 'Maybe Father can help me, if he isn't too far gone from beetroot schnapps.'

As he ran along the alley he heard galloping footsteps behind him in the darkness and was shoved so hard in the small of the back that he was nearly thrown to the ground. But keeping his footing and running on the boy turned to see the zebra from Talbor's menagerie forcing its way past, followed close behind by a peculiar humped creature that I am told is known as a llama. As the animals overtook him, the boy emerged from the alley and ran fast along Marshal Podovsky Street, keeping to the shadows, until he reached the Old Chop House.

'Your father's not here,' said the Tavern Keeper as the Locksmith's Boy leant against the bar, gasping and spluttering for air. 'You've just missed the old drunk. He's gone back home to your mother. Though why he'd risk that, I can't tell—'

Suddenly the door burst open and the Vigils forced their way through the tavern, seizing tankards from terrified drinkers and draining them to the dregs. Plates were hurled to the floor and dogs growled, retreating beneath the tables.

'Out the back,' urged the Tavern Keeper. 'There's a room where you can hide. I'll try to keep the Vigils out, but I can make no promises.'

Ducking from sight the Locksmith's Boy crawled along the floor, through sticky slops of schnapps and rye beer, making his way towards an open doorway at the back of the tavern. Shutting the door behind him, he strained his eyes to see. He was in a small room, used to store old tankards and bottles of beetroot schnapps. There was an empty cupboard with an open door and the boy was preparing to hide inside when a grinning face, framed by black raven feathers, loomed out at him from the shadows. He inhaled sharply and felt behind him for the door handle, preparing to run again, when the figure raised his hand.

'Wait!' he hissed. He pulled back his raven-head mask and a familiar face peered out, blinking in the gloom.

'Alesander!' gasped the Locksmith's Boy.

Alesander clamped his hand over the boy's mouth. 'Don't speak another word,' he whispered. 'I thought you'd come to find your father. I gave Glattburg the slip and ran here as quick as I could. You have to get away from the city.'

'Where will I go?' asked the Locksmith's Boy. 'Schwartzgarten is my home.'

'Go to some far-off place where Talbor can never find you,' said Alesander. 'If you make it past the city walls, follow the river through the forest and beyond – that way you can swim for your life if you come across wolves or bears.'

The Locksmith's Boy nodded.

'Now, quickly,' continued Alesander, leading the boy towards a small door at the back of the room. 'Get out of the city as quickly as you can and never return.'

'Thank you...' began the Locksmith's Boy. But there was no more time to talk.

Alesander opened the door a crack and peered out to

make certain the dark alley beyond was free of Vigils. 'It's safe,' he whispered, and watched as the Locksmith's Boy slipped away without a backward glance.

The boy ran for all he was worth, heading towards the River Schwartz, darting in and out of narrow streets and alleyways to avoid capture. He headed for cover along the wide pathway that ran behind the Emperor Xavier Hotel. 'Perhaps I can climb down from the high river wall to the bank below,' he thought. 'Then I can follow the river out of the city without being seen.'

But as he climbed up on the wall that bordered the roaring River Schwartz below, a voice called out to him, 'And where do you think you're going, raven killer?'

The Locksmith's Boy turned. There, on the pathway below him, stood a lone Vigil. The boy took a pace backwards.

'Not another step more,' said the Vigil, a fat man with a voice like a bear. He raised his gun and pointed it at the Locksmith's Boy. 'Move again and I'll shoot.'

And what would you have done, given the choice, reader? Face a hanging on the orders of the tyrant Emeté Talbor? Jump to your certain death in the surging waters of the River Schwartz? Or risk a bullet in your head? Nor did the Locksmith's Boy know what to do.

The Vigil threw back his head and gave the raven cry. An answering caw came back at once from a nearby street.

The Locksmith's Boy took another step backwards on the wall and the Vigil laughed. 'I warned you, boy.' He cocked the trigger of his gun, and as he did so there was a stamping and a snorting, and the rhinoceros from Talbor's menagerie appeared on the pathway.

Before he could utter another cry, the Vigil was trampled underfoot by the rampaging beast.

There was nothing for it. The Locksmith's Boy turned, took a deep breath and dived from the wall, dropping like a stone into the River Schwartz far below.

How Kalvitas Gained His Name

━━━◆◆◆━━━

THE LOCKSMITH'S Boy must surely be dead, you will say, dashed to death on the jagged rocks of the River Schwartz, or drowned within an inch of his life and then drowned another inch more. And perhaps you have been thinking that a lowly Locksmith's Boy is a character who can happily go to his watery grave without doing a jot of harm to the story I am relating. Well, that shows what you know.

So here is the Locksmith's Boy again, alive but only just, struggling to the surface of the foaming river and gasping for air. His life was flashing before him, but as the boy was only thirteen it flashed all the quicker. At just the point where dying seemed the most sensible thing to do, a wooden crate washed past, and he clutched at it desperately.

To be precise in the telling of the story, the boy *imagined* he was clutching at a wooden crate, for it was, in fact, an empty coffin, thick with green algae.

It was a battle for the Locksmith's Boy to cling on and keep his head above water as he was tossed around in the darkness by the swiftly flowing river. He was swept under the Old Orlaf Bridge and far beyond the forest outside the great city, carried along on the surging tide of water.

The next thing the boy remembered was waking on the banks of the River Schwartz, still clinging onto the coffin. Though he could not have guessed it, he was more than one hundred kilometres downstream of the city of Schwartzgarten. His eyes flickered open and he squinted in the bright morning light. Perched perilously on the mountainside which rose steeply from the river, and towering many hundreds of feet above him, were the imposing grey turrets of Prince Alberto's Summer Palace.

He could make out trees on the far bank of the river and a spindly plume of grey smoke as it curled up through the spruce branches from a distant chimney. Then his eyes closed once more, and he slipped into unconsciousness.

Sometime later, he became aware of a stabbing pain in his side and then the sound of a girl's voice.

'Prod him again,' said the voice.

The Locksmith's Boy kept his eyes tight shut. He was paralysed by fear. 'Surely,' he thought, 'I will be arrested as a spy. And then what?'

'Frederick's found a dead body,' said the girl.

The Locksmith's Boy heard a man grunting as he climbed slowly down from the riverbank.

'How do you know he's dead?' asked the man.

'He looks dead,' said a boy's voice – this was Frederick, the Locksmith's Boy presumed.

To make certain that the figure was indeed dead, Frederick prodded again with a long stick and the Locksmith's Boy groaned. The girl gasped and Frederick jumped back in surprise, tripping over a rock and falling hard on his behind.

'We must take him with us,' said the man. 'There is still life in him.'

At last, the Locksmith's Boy opened his eyes.

'What's your name?' whispered the man, lifting the boy gently into a rowing boat that bobbed nearby. His face was round and red, his eyes burned as bright as gas lamps and his breath was sweet like marzipan.

The Locksmith's Boy stared back blankly and the man shook his head.

'Can't speak, or don't want to?'

Frederick pointed to the shattered coffin that lay beside the boy. On the lid was an engraved brass plaque. 'Look. There's a name. "M. KALVITAS".'

The man nodded. 'Strange,' he said, 'to arrive by coffin. Most people come by boat.' He laughed. 'Then that's what we shall call you, boy. Kalvitas.'

The man rowed the boat downstream to a pony and cart which stood on a dirt track beside the river. With Frederick's help he lifted the Locksmith's Boy onto an empty sack, beside a basket of wild mushrooms that had been gathered from the riverbank.

The cart rattled slowly up the steep path towards the Summer Palace, following a crystal stream, which was fed by a mountain spring. The path wound its way through a small town, with buildings of slate and thatch, and the boy lowered his head so he would not be seen. The air was thinner than his lungs were used to, and he gasped to gain his breath. All the time the girl watched him. She was beautiful, with plaited blonde hair and piercing blue eyes – but she scowled whenever the Locksmith's Boy turned his face towards her.

'Where do you come from, boy?' asked the man, as he urged his pony onwards up the steepening hill.

'Far away,' said the boy quietly.

'If you won't tell, I won't ask again,' said the man, with a laugh. 'My name is Klaus. Most people call me the Pastry Chef.'

'Why?' asked Kalvitas.

'Because he's a pastry chef in the palace kitchens,' said Frederick sourly. 'That's why.'

The cart turned a corner and Kalvitas gasped as ahead of them stood the high grey walls of the Summer Palace. The golden cupola of the highest tower glinted in the sunlight and the boy held a hand to his eyes.

'That's where we're going,' said the Pastry Chef.

As they approached the gates of the palace the man called out to be admitted. A guard appeared. He was a soldier in the Imperial Army and wore a uniform that Kalvitas knew well from his lead soldiers.

'Who's that you've got there, Pastry Chef?' asked the guard. 'It was just you, Elka and Frederick who set out from the palace. So who's he?'

Kalvitas stiffened as the guard stared suspiciously at him. 'Will I be found out?' he thought. 'Will I be locked up as a spy?'

'This is Kalvitas,' said the Pastry Chef with a laugh. 'You must know Kalvitas. He scrubs the floors in the kitchens.'

Elka smirked and Frederick pinched her on the arm.

The guard shrugged, the gates were opened and the cart rolled on, over the cobbles towards the kitchens of the palace.

The Locksmith's Boy smiled to himself. He had never had a name to call his own; now here was a man handing him 'Kalvitas' on a plate.

It was a name that might belong to a hero.

For a history entitled *The Lily-Livered Prince* it may seem peculiar indeed that I have not yet introduced a character of this name. But I am the one telling the story and not you, so I shall do so the way I see fit. However, as it suits my purpose to do so now, that is precisely what I shall do.

The Lily-Livered Prince, as I choose to call him, was known at this stage in the tale as Prince Eugene, son and heir to Brave Prince Alberto.

Imagine a prince who was fierce as a bull and as cunning as a snake, a prince with the wit of the wisest of generals, a prince beloved of all men.

Prince Eugene was not such a prince. He was a fat boy of sixteen, quite unlike the slim young prince portrayed in flattering paintings of the time. But artists sometimes lie and I do not. He was fair-haired and had long and delicate fingers. The Prince was over-fond of cakes and pastries – he was idle and too much in love with himself to be of use to anybody. And he blinked like an owl when worry afflicted his mind, as it often did, and this was disagreeable to all who knew him.

Prince Eugene liked poems and mechanical things, and was good at heart. But like most boys with an interest in poetry, he was also an idiot.

So let us meet this unfortunate prince. In the music

room, high above the palace kitchens, he had spent an enjoyable morning at his studies. The Court Composer, Constantin Esterburg (noted author of the book *The Virtue of the Violin*) had entertained Prince Eugene with a new musical composition for strings, entitled *Wolves of the Forest Roar and Run*. However, like most of Constantin's compositions, it had not been completed – such is the way with true artists.

Ottoburg, the Court Inventor, had taught the Prince of the sun and the stars, presenting the boy with a brass cosmological clock that could be wound by a key to illustrate the movement of the planets.

Next came Vincenzo, a tall and kindly man who had been engaged by Prince Alberto to instruct his son in the art of war, as all princes should be educated. Vincenzo considered war beneath him, preferring instead to talk of art and poetry, but as the Tutor had fallen on hard times and had not a curseling to his name when he arrived at the Summer Palace, he agreed to teach the young Prince whatever Prince Alberto wished him to be taught.

'War,' said the Tutor with a sigh, 'is the art of transforming man into meat.'

Prince Eugene frowned. 'Though I was not yet born when my family escaped from Schwartzgarten, I remember the tales that were told of my father's brave battles against Emeté Talbor and the Dark Count. And I knew then, Vincenzo, that I would not grow up to become a soldier. Swords are heavy and blood is messy. Perhaps Fate has marked me out for better things than battle.'

'Fate doesn't mark us out,' replied the Tutor sadly. 'Everything in this life is ordered according to logic. Now, we must talk of tactics, as your father wishes.'

'I don't want to talk any more of Talbor or his soldiers,' groaned Prince Eugene, blinking hard. 'I want to read to you from the new book that I have written.'

'Very well,' said Vincenzo, who was enough of a tactician to know when he was beaten. 'As Your Highness pleases.'

Prince Eugene smiled. He slipped a small volume from his pocket and turned the crisp pages until he found his place.

'It is a book on manners,' he announced and began to read.

HOW TO EAT PASTRIES MOST PROPERLY

from the honest pen of Prince Eugene

———◆·◆·◆———

CHAPTER ONE – EATING TIDILY WITH A FORK AND SPOON

Do not clutch your pastry by the crust. That is very ill-mannered. Secure the pastry with the tip of your fork. Then, with your spoon, cut away a little of the pastry. Using the tines of your fork, push the morsel of pastry onto your spoon. Open your mouth, but do not open it too widely. Manoeuvre the spoon carefully inside and allow the pastry to slip smoothly onto your eager tongue. As soon as the tip of the spoon has been removed from your mouth, close it. It is unmannerly to chew pastries with your mouth wide open.

'Are there many chapters?' asked Vincenzo, as Prince Eugene licked his finger and turned to the next page.

There were indeed many chapters and the Tutor listened patiently to each and every one. It was not a disagreeable task, as Vincenzo had perfected the art of sleeping with his eyes half-open and nodding at appropriate moments. As soon as the Prince finished his recital, he presented his tutor with a copy of the book, which he had dedicated to Vincenzo.

As Prince Eugene left his tutor for the day, he set off towards his bedchamber, passing full-length portraits of his royal forebears. Paintings of his father, Crown Prince Alberto, hung everywhere about the palace, picturing him as a brave soldier, trampling the enemy underfoot on his horse, or goring the enemy to death with a bayonet, or blowing the enemy sky-high with cannon fire.

If you have not visited the Schwartzgarten Museum, or if your parents are too miserly to buy you history books of the great city, then I suppose it falls to me to conjure up a portrait of Crown Prince Alberto and Princess Aurelia, Prince Eugene's mother.

Prince Alberto was an imposing man with dark eyes and a red nose, and seemed to his son the sort of fearful creature that a boy might search for beneath his bed before blowing out the candle for sleep. Princess Aurelia was a small and slender woman and had something of the wolf about her – a narrowness of the eyes, a sharpness of the teeth. Is this the sort of portrait you would wish to have hanging from your wall, reader? No, I imagine it is not.

As is the case with most parents, Prince Alberto and Princess Aurelia came to hate their son more and more with each passing year. Sometimes weeks would go by without a word passing between Prince Eugene and his parents. And this was the way the Prince liked it. So it was with dismay that he rounded a corner to find his father looming before him.

'Oh, it's you,' said Prince Alberto, in much the same way as a man might exclaim, 'Ah, a cockroach!' before bringing down his boot and crushing the insect to dust.

'Yes, Father,' said Prince Eugene apologetically. 'It is me.'

'What has Vincenzo been teaching you today, boy?' enquired Prince Alberto. 'About slicing with your sword and chopping off arms and legs, I hope?'

Prince Eugene shifted nervously on the spot and his eyes blinked. 'No, Father,' he replied weakly.

'Then what?' roared Prince Alberto.

'I have been reading to him from my book of manners,' said Prince Eugene.

'Manners?' screamed Prince Alberto. '*Manners!*'

Prince Alberto had no love for books on manners, no love for poetry, no love for art. As far as Prince Eugene was concerned, his father had very little brain indeed.

'Go back to Vincenzo at once, you snivelling waste of a head!' bellowed Prince Alberto. 'The man must teach you to become a soldier!'

'I pity you,' said the young prince, flushing with anger and blinking harder than ever. 'Because you're a stupid man, Father. And you know nothing of art and beauty and...and the way to eat pastries most properly.'

Prince Alberto seized his son by the throat, lifting him from the ground. His eyes were bloodshot with fury and his eyebrows stood out as white as clouds against the blueness of his face.

Prince Eugene wriggled and kicked, but he could not free himself from his father's vice-like grip. 'I'm sorry,' he gasped. 'I'm sorry!'

It was only when the air seemed to splutter from Prince Eugene's lungs that his father finally released him, and he fell to the ground like a fat puppet whose strings had been cut.

Crown Prince Alberto directed the full force of his

glare at the cowering young prince and his voice dropped to an ominous bass note that trembled like the strings of Constantin's violin.

'Call me stupid again, boy, and I'll knock your block off.'

IN THE KITCHENS OF THE SUMMER PALACE

I F YOU have read my book *Recipes from the North-Eastern Region of the Country*, and pored for hours over the hand-tinted illustrations, then you will know the kitchens of the Summer Palace well – the high barrelled ceiling, the floor of polished slate, the marble counters, the vast ovens where cakes and pastries were baked and the rows of copper pans and moulds that glittered in the lamplight. If you have not read my book, then you will have to use your imagination.

The Locksmith's Boy (who had now tried out the name of Kalvitas and found it to his liking) gazed about him in wonder as battalions of cooks in white uniforms scuttled backwards and forwards, feeding the fires for the ovens, rolling out sheets of paper-thin pastry, tending to simmering pans that bubbled and rattled on the enormous stoves.

Elka smiled and passed Kalvitas a dish. 'Here. Eat,' she said. 'You look like you're half-starved.'

'Thank you,' said Kalvitas, smiling back at the girl as

he ate hungrily from the bowl of sweet-sour cherry and almond streusel, drenched with rich, mountain cream.

'There's more where that came from,' said the Pastry Chef, melting chocolate in a copper bowl and stirring in cream from a large jug. 'You eat quickly for a corpse out of his coffin!'

Frederick hurried up with a cake pan, and the Pastry Chef pressed his finger against the dense chocolate torte inside.

'Good, Frederick,' said the Pastry Chef. 'Now tip it out onto the slab.'

Frederick carefully released the torte onto the marble counter and the Pastry Chef spread it thickly with warm cloudberry jam, before covering it with the melted chocolate. 'We use a dove feather as a brush,' explained the Pastry Chef, as he carefully smoothed the chocolate. 'Real love goes into pastry-making. This is for Prince Eugene. The boy likes his desserts.'

But Kalvitas was more interested in Elka, smiling as he watched her set about her work.

'Elka is a stray,' said Frederick sharply, noticing that Kalvitas could hardly take his eyes from the girl. Frederick was a sickly-looking boy, pale, with grey eyes and a face permanently set in a frown. 'She was a foundling girl.'

'Shut up,' said Elka. 'I have as much right to be here as you do.'

'One day she will be mine,' hissed Frederick under his breath, whisking in cream to thicken a lingonberry mousse, all the time watching Kalvitas from the corner of his eye.

The Pastry Chef reached out to take the bowl from Kalvitas and exclaimed, 'Your hands are as cold as the grave, boy!'

'Is that bad?' asked Kalvitas.

'No, no,' said the man. 'It's good. It's very good. We need cold hands for working chocolate.'

'And Frederick has sweaty hands,' laughed Elka.

Frederick scowled.

'Here,' said the Pastry Chef, passing Kalvitas a long, flat knife and pointing towards a pool of chocolate that had set hard on the marble counter. 'Hold the knife like this and drag it slowly across the chocolate.'

Kalvitas did as he was told, and as he pulled the knife across the surface of the chocolate, a long and elegant curl began to form.

'You're a natural,' laughed the Pastry Chef. 'Even Frederick can't do that well, and he's my own flesh and blood.'

'Frederick is your son?' asked Kalvitas.

'Yes,' replied Frederick scornfully. 'Though you'd hardly know it.'

'A boy has to earn his father's admiration,' said the Pastry Chef with a frown, finishing the torte with the curls of chocolate that Kalvitas had so skilfully fashioned, and dusting the dessert with the finest cocoa. Kalvitas watched in awe as the beautiful creation was carried away from the kitchens to the table of Prince Eugene.

It seemed at once to Kalvitas that this was the place where he most desired to be, for the time being at least, especially as it would mean spending his days with the beautiful Elka. He still dreamed of being a hero in battle, of course, but a hero's journey can take many paths.

⸻◆⸻

As the passing days turned to weeks, Kalvitas learnt many tasks in the kitchen: filling piping bags, heating chocolate in copper pans and mixing the bubbling vats of sugar fondant. And in time the Pastry Chef trusted Kalvitas more and more: to top a chocolate torte with elegant swirls of piped cream, or fill the vast copper moulds with mousses and jellies. He even trusted the boy to make spun sugar, watching like a father as Kalvitas allowed the soft strands of silken caramel to drizzle down onto the back of an oiled ladle.

It was clear that Kalvitas had a talent with chocolate, and the Pastry Chef would set him to work preparing sweetmeats for the Imperial table. Sometimes the Pastry Chef would even trust him to make small pastries for Prince Eugene.

'Bake me something special,' he said one day. 'Show me what you're made of, boy.'

Searching for inspiration, Kalvitas remembered the eagle pastries that had been served at Old Engelfried's table, and rolled out pastry which he filled with chocolate and marzipan, before twisting the pastry into shape to resemble a small bird.

'Who made this?' demanded Prince Eugene, having hurried down into the kitchens brandishing a wing of the chocolate and marzipan eagle, little more than half an hour after the dish of pastries had been sent to his room.

'Well, go on, boy,' said the Pastry Chef. 'Speak up.'

Kalvitas shuffled forward. 'It was me,' he mumbled.

'And what is your name?' asked the Prince.

'They call me Kalvitas,' replied the boy.

'Such flavours,' said the Prince, closing his eyes in delight. 'Where did you learn to bake that way?'

'From my home, a long way off,' said Kalvitas, still not wanting to admit that he was from Schwartzgarten.

'So delicious,' murmured Prince Eugene. 'A rhapsody in pastry form. You will bake a tray of them for me each afternoon and bring them to me yourself.'

Friendships can form quickly, but nothing unites two people quicker than a love of fine pastries. And I have eaten enough pastries in my time to know this to be true.

Prince Eugene was starved of friends at the Summer Palace and was anxious to spend as little time with his mother and father as possible. So instead he spent his afternoons with Kalvitas, discussing recipes that might tempt and tantalise him. Within a week, Prince Eugene had declared Kalvitas the wisest person in the whole palace.

Frederick could scarce believe the speed with which

Kalvitas mastered the art of pastry-making. They shared a small room together in a high turret of the palace, and Frederick watched Kalvitas closely as, night after night, by the flame of his candle, the boy pored over ancient recipes, committing the ingredients to memory and dreaming up ever more elaborate desserts for the Prince. Kalvitas had a talent for invention; that much was clear. And Frederick despised him for it.

———•———

As the seasons changed and the golden days of autumn slowly died, it was time to begin stockpiling food to see the palace through the long winter months. Small avalanches of snow would often slip from the mountainside, making the Summer Palace inaccessible to all but the most adventurous of merchant travellers. But there were stores of tinned food and salted meat, and always a plentiful supply of sugar, and nobody in the palace would ever have to starve.

Kalvitas was slow to grow accustomed to the cold mountain air, which was many degrees cooler than the air of Schwartzgarten. His face was red and cracked by the wind.

'This palace was never meant for the winter,' said the Pastry Chef one day as he struggled with Kalvitas to heave a sack of flour across the courtyard to the kitchens. 'It was built so the Imperial Family could escape the summer heat of Schwartzgarten. They liked the cool air here.'

'Have you ever been to Schwartzgarten?' asked Kalvitas, his teeth chattering from the cold.

'Not me,' said the Pastry Chef. 'I'm a country boy. But I hear tell it's a wondrous place. I should like to visit the great city before I die.'

<hr />

Though the Summer Palace had many courtiers and advisers, two are of most importance to this story – Kayakovsky and Bagelbof. Kayakovsky was a tall and learned man, who spent so much of his time bowing that he had become permanently hunched. He was a good man; that is beyond dispute.

Bagelbof was a more brooding presence in the Palace, though loyal and true. A soldier in his youth, he was short and dark, with eyebrows so thick his eyes were almost hidden from view.

Kayakovsky and Bagelbof now enter our stage and bow in humble greeting to the reader.

Though Prince Alberto had weathered many winters at the Summer Palace, it seemed that the ice and snow had finally entered his very soul. Too weak to stand, he was confined to his bed, little more than a ghost of his former self.

Prince Eugene sat at his father's bedside, watching the sun through the window as it slowly clawed its way into the blue morning sky. Kayakovsky remained at a respectful distance. Where Bagelbof was, I could not tell you.

Prince Alberto stirred in his bed, gazing blindly at his son through milky eyes. 'Who is it?' he croaked. 'Who's there?'

'It is I, Father,' said the Prince. 'Eugene. Your only son.'

'Is no one else here to watch over me?'

'There is Kayakovsky, Father.'

'I am bored with Kayakovsky,' said Prince Alberto. 'You will have to do, I suppose.' He beckoned his son forward. 'Have you ever seen a dead body, boy?'

'No, Father,' replied Prince Eugene.

Prince Alberto shook his head in despair. 'To reach your

age, and never to see a corpse,' he croaked. 'It's enough to make a man weep.'

'It's not as though there are corpses lying here and there around the palace,' thought Prince Eugene moodily. And yet he said, 'What is it like, Father? To see a dead body?'

'It's like staring at a wax figure,' replied his father. 'It's a shell, nothing more. The spark has gone.'

'Ah,' replied Prince Eugene, who could think of nothing better to say.

Prince Alberto's peace was disturbed by the clatter of carriage wheels on the cobbles outside the palace. 'Too loud!' he roared, before sinking back against the pillows. 'Too loud.'

On Prince Eugene's order, the cobbles were immediately strewn with straw to muffle the iron wheels and horses' hooves.

The carriage that disturbed Prince Alberto had arrived at the palace from Schwartzgarten, bearing Ambassador Volkoff. He entered the Grand Hall with its vast vaulted ceiling and floor of red and black Tanevan marble and looked about him. How he wished the palace was his; his moustache twitched at the thought.

Descending the staircase from his father's bedchamber,

Prince Eugene stepped forward to greet the Ambassador. He did not like Volkoff, but he feared the dark glint in the man's eye and always thought it safer to be polite.

'You have returned to us, cousin.'

'You honour me with your greeting, Highness,' replied Volkoff with a thin smile. He clicked his heels and gave a low bow.

Princess Aurelia entered from the breakfast room.

'Mother,' said Prince Eugene, 'my dear cousin Volkoff is here.'

'You think yourself a page now, not a prince?' said Princess Aurelia, scowling at her son. 'To introduce every guest to the palace?'

'It saddened me to hear that Prince Alberto has been taken sick,' said Ambassador Volkoff. 'I set out from Schwartzgarten the very moment news arrived.'

Princess Aurelia inclined her head and offered her hand, which the Ambassador dutifully bowed to kiss.

'Like the son I never had,' she murmured softly, as Volkoff raised his head and smiled.

Prince Eugene coughed politely. 'But you did have a son, Mother,' he reminded her. 'You had me.'

The Princess turned and glowered at the Prince and he shrank back, as if attempting to blend in with the wallpaper.

———

Time passed and though Crown Prince Alberto grew no better, he grew no worse. Winter turned to spring, and while Alberto lay in bed the Dowager Princess ruled in his place, with Volkoff to advise her. And Prince Eugene was happy to let his mother rule.

But Alberto grew suddenly sicker, as if to spite the Court Physician (who had predicted a full recovery), and Prince Eugene was awoken in the middle of the night by a gentle but insistent knock at the door of his bedchamber.

'Come,' said the Prince, sitting up in bed.

Kayakovsky entered the room. His face was grey and his back was more hunched than usual, as though the weight of the world rested on his shoulders.

'What is it?' asked Prince Eugene, hiding his shaking hands in the folds of the eiderdown. He was not ready to become Crown Prince, and yet he knew the moment was fast drawing near.

'It is time,' said Kayakovsky.

Prince Eugene quickly pulled on his dressing gown and slippers. With Kayakovsky at his side he hurried along the polished marble passageways of the palace until he reached his father's chamber.

Princess Aurelia stood at the foot of the bed, as pale and silent as a statue on a tomb. Volkoff stood beside her, dressed entirely in black and smoothing his moustache with his fingertips, lost in thought. Bagelbof stood at the head of the bed, where Prince Alberto was propped up against two overstuffed pillows. The Court Physician held a cold compress to the Crown Prince's forehead.

Prince Eugene felt sick to the pit of his stomach as he approached his father's bedside. The Court Physician bowed and stepped back. Every breath seemed to crackle from Prince Alberto's throat and he grasped for his son's hand.

'What is it, Father?' whispered Prince Eugene. 'Do you want Mother?'

'No,' gasped Prince Alberto. 'I want you, curse it!'

'Why me?' asked the young prince. 'Are you delirious, Father?'

Summoning what little strength he had remaining,

Prince Alberto pushed himself up from the bed so he could whisper in his son's ear.

'There...there is a secret you must know,' he panted.

'That you love me, Father?' whispered Prince Eugene.

'No, no, you fool,' hissed Prince Alberto and pressed a small golden key into the palm of his son's hand. 'Gutterfink...*Gutterfink*...'

Prince Eugene stared in surprise at his father. The word was entirely alien to him. 'Gutter-what?'

But Prince Alberto did not utter another word. He fell back against the pillows as a death rattle of air escaped his lungs in short, sickening rasps. The light was extinguished in his eyes.

'The Prince is dead,' whispered the Court Physician, gently closing the man's eyelids.

Kayakovsky was struggling to remove the Imperial signet ring from Prince Alberto's dead hand. 'His fingers are swollen,' he mumbled apologetically. 'I can't seem to remove it. We'll just work it off, with a bit of warm butter to grease it.'

Prince Eugene shuddered and turned to leave, slipping the golden key in the pocket of his dressing gown.

'Your Majesty,' said Bagelbof. He made a deep bow and whispered, 'Prince Alberto is dead. Long live Crown Prince Eugene!'

Even Princess Aurelia managed a low curtsy, though she was grinding her teeth as she did so. From this point in the tale she will be referred to as the Dowager or the Dowager Princess, for this was her title after the death of her husband, Prince Alberto. And death hung eternally about her, worn tightly round her shoulders as some might wear an ermine cape.

It was not yet light and Prince Eugene walked gloomily back to his rooms. He trudged slowly along the dark passageways, staring up at the familiar oil paintings of his royal forebears. At every corner of the palace there stood a cowering courtier.

'Prince Alberto is dead. Long live Crown Prince Eugene!'

'Yes, yes, yes,' said Prince Eugene, stopping at a painting of a long-dead ancestor which hung high on the wall in front of him. The figure in the portrait wore a powdered wig, as was the custom in his day, and appeared scarcely older than Prince Eugene himself.

Below the painting was a glass dome, resting on a golden stand, a reliquary which housed the grinning skull of his royal relation. Prince Eugene lifted the dome, and from the cushion of scarlet satin, plucked the fragile skull, which had been preserved to show the hole from the musket ball that had struck the man dead. The Prince gave the skull a gentle shake and the lead ball clattered about inside, like a dried pea in a baby's rattle.

'Life is short and life is miserable,' sighed Prince Eugene, and returned the relic to its dome, imagining his own skull under glass in the years to come.

CROWN PRINCE EUGENE

———◆❖◆———

IT WAS an Imperial tradition that the son and heir should occupy the chambers of his father on the night of the latter's death. Prince Alberto's body was removed, the bed linen was changed, and Prince Eugene spent his first night in his father's bed – though he did not sleep well, of that you can be sure. Prince Alberto had left a deep impression in the duck feather mattress and Prince Eugene was almost hidden inside the hole. Why they did not change the mattress, I cannot tell you.

Meanwhile, the possessions of the Dowager Princess were taken in crates to a high turret in the north wing of the palace, with a room for her maid, a lumpen girl named Monette.

A corpse-sculptor had prepared a death mask of Prince Alberto and the grim memento was cast in lead and presented to the Dowager Princess. She ran her pale fingers over the lifeless, leaden face of her late husband.

Volkoff, who had not yet returned to Schwartzgarten, watched as Monette hung the likeness of Prince Alberto from a hook on the wall, alongside the death masks of the Dowager Princess's mother and father.

The room was lit by flickering candle flame, the better to suit the Dowager's sallow complexion, and she gazed unhappily at her reflection in the mirror.

'Raven claws,' she sighed, pulling at the folds of paper-thin skin that had gathered at the corner of each eye. 'I grow old while that fool, my son, grows fat. And now *he* is ruler.'

It was such a thought that had been occupying the mind of the devious Volkoff as he sat and pulled the leather gauntlets from his hands. It was entirely agreeable to him that Prince Alberto was dead, but it was necessary that Prince Eugene should follow his father into the grave as quickly as was possible.

'Banished to rot in my chambers!' cried the Dowager, sipping a mouthful of tea and swilling it around as if the very taste disgusted her. 'Something must be done about my son.'

Ambassador Volkoff smiled a dark smile. 'According to the Act of Succession,' he replied smoothly, with the oily charm that only an ambassador could muster, 'if Prince

Eugene were to die before producing an heir, then the throne would naturally pass to his mother.'

The Dowager pondered this. 'If he were to die.' The words dripped deliciously from her tongue. 'What a pleasing thought.'

———

The next morning a telegram arrived from Prince Alberto's brother, the Archduke Dmitri.

```
Tell Alberto not to die until I arrive STOP
```

Prince Eugene let out a low moan. He did not like his uncle and the prospect of the Archduke's imminent arrival filled him with little joy. There was a second telegram, despatched minutes later. Prince Eugene groaned as he read the message.

```
But if the obstinate pig ignores my telegram
and dies anyway do not bury him STOP
Arriving tomorrow STOP Wish to see Alberto
before lowered into ground STOP Make quite
```

```
sure dead and not sleeping STOP Cut head off

if necessary STOP
```

—•—

The following day an outrider appeared on horseback to announce the approach of his master.

'The Archduke has arrived!' cried the Master-at-Arms and the mighty gates to the palace were thrown open.

A carriage, bearing the arms of the Imperial Family, rattled up over the cobbles. The door swung open and the Archduke jumped out before the wheels had even ground to a halt. He was a tall and handsome man, with a flop of greying blond hair. His shoulders were so broad and his chest so puffed out that his head seemed too small for his body. He strode up the palace steps into the Grand Hall and removed his cape, flinging it with such force into the arms of a waiting footman that the man stumbled backwards into an ornamental suit of armour.

'There you are,' bellowed the Archduke, holding a monocle to his eye as he spotted Prince Eugene attempting to conceal himself behind a table. 'Well, crawl out of the woodwork, you little worm, and greet your uncle.'

Prince Eugene did as he was told.

'You've grown,' said the Archduke.

The Prince smiled. 'Taller, you mean?'

'Fatter,' replied his uncle, embracing his nephew.

'You're squeezing the air out of me,' gasped Prince Eugene.

'About time too,' declared the Archduke. 'Someone should have stuck a pin in you an age ago.'

It was often difficult to tell for certain when the Archduke was being humorous and when he was not.

'Good honest food, that's what you need,' the Archduke continued. 'Not the sweets and pastries you shovel into that fat face of yours. So have some creature killed at once and see that it's roasted well.'

Pushing aside a servant who was attempting to carry his luggage, the Archduke made his way quickly up the marble staircase, his footsteps echoing with a thunderous boom.

'So my brother's dead, is he?' said the Archduke as the Dowager Princess approached. 'What were his last words? Something about food, were they?'

He gave a barking laugh and the Dowager Princess attempted a smile, though it pained her to do so. How she wished it was the Archduke at rest in his coffin and not her beloved husband.

The Archduke was taken to view Prince Alberto's open casket, squinting hard through his monocle at the corpse of his brother. The mouth of the unfortunate monarch had been set in a skewed and chilling smile.

'I haven't seen him look so healthy these past ten years,' said the Archduke. 'Or have the morticians got to him? Coloured his cheeks, have they? Smeared him over with corpse-wax?'

'The colour is quite natural,' said the Dowager coldly.

'Excellent, excellent,' said the Archduke. 'Good blood. The Imperial Family has always been a healthy family. Even in his tomb Alberto will look heartier than most men living.'

Visitors From Offelmarkstein

———◆·✦·◆———

THE NEXT day the citizens of the town below the Summer Palace arrived to pay tribute to the dead prince, wailing as they climbed the winding cobbled street – though it was not the death of Prince Alberto that was the cause of the wailing, but the steepness of the hill.

The coffin was carried into the Grand Hall by the tallest members of the Imperial Army, and out into the courtyard where the funeral could be witnessed by the gathered townspeople. The Dowager Princess followed behind her brave and beloved husband's coffin, hooded in a black cape with Monette gathering her train of black lace. Then came Prince Eugene, smiling nervously as he passed Kalvitas and the Pastry Chef. They bowed in respect to the new Crown Prince.

Ambassador Volkoff seemed much affected by Prince Alberto's demise, burying his face in a large pocket handkerchief. But truth be told, as must be the case in all good history books, Volkoff did not shed a single tear for Alberto. In his mind he had crossed a neat line through the late prince's name as he clawed his way ever closer to the Crown. The thought amused him and hiding his face in a handkerchief was the only way to stifle his merriment without revealing his true feelings to the court.

Kayakovsky, Bagelbof and the Archduke looked on in silence as the Master-at-Arms stood at the head of the coffin, reading from the ancient words laid down in the *Imperial Book of the Dead*.

'As you emerged from the dust and were made man,
so you shall be returned to dust.'

'I wish Father was still with us,' said Prince Eugene, staring down at his reflection in his polished boots.

And this was quite true. But you must understand, reader, that though Prince Eugene cared little more for his father than his father had cared for him, he would have been happier if it was Alberto's behind warming the throne and not his own.

The Dowager Princess did not reply, though her eyes burned fiercely. Her hatred for her son had grown and grown, eating away inside her like the worm in the fruit.

Though Prince Eugene had not quite reached his seventeenth birthday, a date had already been set for his coronation.

'And the boy must take a wife,' said Bagelbof to Kayakovsky. 'Someone of wealth. A girl with a hundred thousand golden mitres or more, to swell the palace coffers.'

'And she must be stupid,' said the Dowager Princess.

'Why stupid, madam?' asked Kayakovsky.

The Dowager Princess smiled. 'Because she is expected to marry my idiot son.'

The week after the burial of Prince Alberto, a page arrived from the Grand Duchy of Offelmarkstein in the north, bearing the likeness of the Grand Duchesses Euphenia and Tatiana. As they were identical twins the Prince was only supplied with a single miniature, a delicate enamel portrait in a small gilt picture frame.

'And is this what they look like?' asked Prince Eugene, squinting at the image of a beautiful girl, with cheeks like rosebuds, hair as golden as corn and eyes as blue as a summer sky. 'What they *really* look like?'

'I am told that it hardly does them justice,' said Kayakovsky.

Prince Eugene stared suspiciously at the man. 'Which means they are both as ugly as sin, I suppose?'

Three days later, a carriage arrived from the north, carrying the Grand Duke of Offelmarkstein and his daughters, the Grand Duchesses Euphenia and Tatiana. The carriage stopped outside the palace and the twin sisters emerged.

Prince Eugene's heart sank. Though the duchesses were indeed identical, they could not have been further from their portrait if the artist had worn a blindfold. They were tall and dark-haired, with long necks, pale faces and pointed chins. Their noses, turned upwards at the tip with flared nostrils, reminded Prince Eugene unfavourably of the basted pig's head that had been served at dinner the night before.

Even the movements of the Grand Duchesses were identical as they advanced slowly across the cobbled courtyard. They towered above the Prince and he crouched before them like a mouse before a snake.

Prince Eugene opened his mouth to speak, but before

he could get a single word out the Grand Duchesses said at once, 'He's not a bit like his portrait.'

Prince Eugene sighed.

Grand Duchess Tatiana and Grand Duchess Euphenia were served cocoa in the palace music room, entertained by Constantin on his violin.

Grand Duchess Tatiana gave a smile that could have curdled milk and muttered under her breath.

'What does she say?' asked the Prince.

'That she is in mourning for our father,' replied Grand Duchess Euphenia.

'But your father is still alive,' said the Prince, gesturing to the elderly Grand Duke of Offelmarkstein, who stood in the corner of the room, secretly slipping beetroot schnapps into his cocoa.

Grand Duchess Tatiana laughed, and her eyes glinted darkly. 'Yes, but *one day* he will be dead.'

The Grand Duke approached and saluted, sloshing cocoa from his cup. 'The Grand Duchesses are my darlings,' he confided to Prince Eugene, as the twin sisters talked with the Archduke. 'They are the very light of my life. If only you could marry them both together.'

'Quite,' said Prince Eugene politely.

'But you can't, can you?' continued the Count, gripping the Prince's arm desperately.

'No,' said Prince Eugene, and quivered at the thought.

'Is there anyone else at the Summer Palace in need of a wife?' asked the Grand Duke. 'Or do you have deep dungeons?' he whispered, draining his cocoa cup. 'Might you be willing to do an old man a good turn?'

In the hour before dinner, Kayakovsky was surprised to discover Prince Eugene cowering beneath a table in the library.

'Are you well, Majesty?' he enquired.

'I'm hiding,' replied Prince Eugene. 'The Grand Duchesses Tatiana and Euphenia chill the very blood in my veins. I don't want to marry either one of the pig-nosed monsters!'

'There are worse fates that can befall a young man, Majesty,' said Kayakovsky with a gentle smile.

'You mean death?' replied the Prince.

Prince Eugene sought out his friend Kalvitas in the palace kitchens, and watched as the boy prepared desserts in honour of the visitors from Offelmarkstein.

'How much easier it must be living life as a pastry boy,' said the Prince.

'How do you mean?' asked Kalvitas, filling a basket of chocolate with marzipan fruits.

'Nobody sends strange twins to marry you, do they?' said the Prince.

'No,' agreed Kalvitas. 'They don't. But then, I'm too young to be married.'

Prince Eugene uttered a plaintive cry. 'And so am I!'

Frederick was busily stirring the contents of a large cauldron and the Prince sniffed hard and winced in disgust.

'What is that you are cooking?' he asked.

'Goulash,' answered Frederick. 'Made to a traditional recipe from Offelmarkstein, Majesty.'

'No wonder the Grand Duchesses are so peculiar if that's the muck they eat,' said Prince Eugene, his eyes watering from the smoky paprika. 'Spicy food does not agree with me.' He shook his head despairingly. 'Your life is so much simpler than mine, Kalvitas. You do not have a wolf for a mother and a brute for an uncle. You cook and you eat and one day you will probably marry the girl...Ilka.'

'Elka,' corrected the girl, scowling as she whisked a bowl of cream for a cloudberry mousse.

'Steady, girl,' murmured the Pastry Chef under his breath.

'Quite,' continued the Prince with a laugh. 'You will marry Elka and all will be well for you.'

'I won't be marrying anyone, and that's that,' said Elka, though her face had coloured and she lowered her head so she could not meet Kalvitas's eye.

———

At dinner, Prince Eugene was flanked by the two Grand Duchesses. His spirits were so unsettled that he could only toy with his food, as his companions giggled and nudged him with their thin and bony elbows.

After a miserable bowl of the spicy goulash from Offelmarkstein, the table was heaped with desserts from the kitchens and the Prince's spirits lifted. Alongside the whipped cloudberry mousse, there was a chocolate soufflé, an iced bombe of churned frozen custard and a tower of caramel pastries.

As Prince Eugene reached out to scoop up a large spoonful of the cloudberry mousse, the Grand Duchesses wagged their fingers at him.

'You will get fat!' said Grand Duchess Euphenia, with a click of her tongue.

'Fatter!' said Grand Duchess Tatiana and giggled.

Prince Eugene glowered at the Grand Duchesses, which made them giggle all the more.

<hr>

'You will have to choose one of them, Majesty,' whispered Bagelbof on the second week of the Grand Duchesses' visit.

The Prince peered imploringly into the man's eyes. 'Must I?'

'Alas, Majesty,' said Kayakovsky, 'you must. The Grand Duchesses bring great wealth with them.'

But the harder the Prince tried to choose a bride, the more difficult the task became – how might a boy choose between one monster and another? It seemed too that there was no way of escaping the Grand Duchesses. Wherever he turned, there they were, watching. Finally, in desperation, Prince Eugene made his choice.

'You, I suppose. Tatiana.'

'I am Euphenia,' corrected the Grand Duchess with another of her unsettling giggles. 'But it is of no matter.' She sighed and held out her hand to the Prince. 'And now we will be married, yes?' she said, with a spasm of the lips which Prince Eugene took for a smile.

'What will happen to your sister?' asked the Prince the next day, as Grand Duchess Tatiana and her father stepped up into their carriage.

'She will return to the Old Country to die,' replied the Grand Duchess Euphenia.

The Prince was moved to hear this. 'You think your sister will die from a broken heart?' he asked gently.

The Grand Duchess gave a brittle laugh. 'No,' she replied. 'Poison. Do not mourn for her,' she added with a smile, revealing blackened teeth that the Prince had not yet noticed. 'We die because we are sad and we die because we are happy. It is the way of the Old Country.'

A proclamation was made that very day. There would be two glorious royal occasions squeezed neatly into one –

a coronation and a wedding. The death by self-poisoning of Grand Duchess Tatiana two days later was yet another reason to rejoice, as it made her twin sister twice as rich as she had been before.

In accordance with custom, until the wedding, Grand Duchess Euphenia remained at the Summer Palace as a guest of the Dowager Princess, demanding that the spicy goulash of the Old Country should be served at table at least once a day. And though she would often search the corridors of the palace for her husband-to-be, Prince Eugene made sure she rarely succeeded in finding him. Sometimes he would even hide in one of the many lavatories of the Summer Palace, with the door locked and an armed sentry outside to protect him. The silence of the lavatory soothed his troubled mind and the luxuriant softness of the lavatory paper soothed his troubled behind.

It is quite usual for a wife to grow weary of her husband after they have been married, but it is unusual for this to occur before their hands are joined in wedded bliss. However, the Grand Duchess was an unusual girl, and grow weary she did. Though it must be said, a lavatory-lurking Prince is hardly likely to fan the flames of romance.

So at night Grand Duchess Euphenia would sit in the library for hours at a stretch, reading from ancient books dedicated to the history and development of assorted instruments of torture. And when she had finished in the library, she would retire to her room to attend to her prized collection of miniature coffins, daintily sewing corpse-cloths to cover the tiny china figures inside. Such was her way – and a peculiar way it was.

The Coronation Of
Prince Eugene

PRINCE EUGENE'S coronation ensemble had been laid out on the bed: his waistcoat, breeches and stockings, and the finest underclothing, woven by the blind weavers of Lake Taneva. The Prince gazed out from his window. Young as he was, he felt as though his life was already nearing an end. In little more than an hour he would become both Crown Prince and husband, and the feelings that welled up inside him were worse than indigestion.

Two thrones had been set at the centre of the palace courtyard and the coronation canopy had been erected above them. The sun reflected brilliantly from the golden cupola on the highest tower of the palace. It was perfect weather for a coronation.

'Their Imperial Highnesses, the Grand Duke and Grand Duchess Bratsky,' called a page from the courtyard far below.

The Prince turned miserably from the window and returned to his writing desk to complete the poem he had been composing.

Wives, who needs them? I do not,
If I had my way they'd all be shot.

Finally he could put things off no longer. He stood and raised his arms, preparing to be dressed by his waiting valet.

Seven pages lurked outside the door as Prince Eugene emerged from his room, resplendent in his tricorn hat with ostrich feather plumes. The pages stood in line to carry the ermine train of his coronation robes, which was nine yards in length and as heavy as a sack of flour.

Prince Eugene appeared from the palace, walking slowly in time to the coronation anthem, composed by Constantin Esterburg. It was a battle for the Prince to keep his eyes from blinking as he surveyed the crowds of onlookers who sat in tight rows within the palace walls.

The generals of the Imperial Army had assembled and stood in attendance. There was brave General Montelmarte, the inventive General Bratislav, the hungry

Grand Duke Mortburg, the vain General Noisette and the ancient Grand Duke Sergei with his ear trumpet. There was another general amongst their number, the valiant Marshal Pfefferberg, but that is a tale for later.

The Prince's uncle, the Archduke, stood frowning beside the Imperial throne, which glittered in the bright sunlight, burnished with gold.

Anxiously, the Prince took his place on the throne, watching as the canopy of ivory silk billowed above him. He turned to Grand Duchess Euphenia, who sat beside him. She wore bejewelled insects of gold and silver at her wrists and a pearl choker around her long, thin neck. He could not help but notice that her elbows seemed bonier than ever.

'Soon we will be man and wife,' she trilled, craning her neck towards the Prince. 'And one day we will have the little children, yes? With the dark hair and the pale faces, and the sad eyes, and the red lips like smears of blood.'

Prince Eugene shuddered at the thought of such terrifying children, but said nothing.

Coronation heralds sounded their trumpets as the Imperial crown was lifted from its golden cushion and placed on Prince Eugene's head, with a smaller crown for Euphenia, who in that moment became his Princess. On his finger he wore the Imperial signet ring that had lately been cut from his father's lifeless hand.

The crown sat heavily on Prince Eugene's head and he fidgeted on his throne.

'Sit upright,' hissed the Dowager Princess, who sat behind her son. 'Remember you have a spine.'

The day after Prince Eugene's coronation, the Archduke set off at dawn to return to his castle in the north. And as his carriage thundered away, the sly Volkoff summoned Bagelbof to his rooms.

'Things are bad in Schwartzgarten,' said the Ambassador. 'Talbor feels threatened by the young prince.'

This was surprising news to anybody who knew Prince Eugene, but still, Bagelbof was worried.

'Talbor fears that Prince Eugene might plan an attack on Schwartzgarten to claim his father's throne,' Volkoff continued. 'I know that Prince Eugene plans no such campaign, but it is important we prove to Talbor that his intentions are peaceful. The Prince should invite Talbor to the Summer Palace.'

Prince Eugene's first reaction to this idea was to hide in a cupboard and not come out. But when Bagelbof convinced the Prince that it was wiser to entertain a guest than face invasion, Prince Eugene reluctantly agreed, even though there was no one in the world that the Prince wished to see less than Émeté Talbor.

Bagelbof sent Volkoff back to Schwartzgarten, inviting Talbor to visit the Summer Palace as guest of Prince Eugene and Princess Euphenia.

'We will have another banquet,' said Prince Eugene, pacing the floor of the palace kitchens as the Pastry Chef and Kalvitas, Frederick and Elka stood in line. 'Cousin Volkoff suggests that an edible palace would be a dessert that might please the tyrant.'

'Which palace, Majesty?' asked the Pastry Chef.

'The tyrant's palace in Schwartzgarten, that was once my father's,' said Prince Eugene, 'with Talbor's raven flag flying above the palace dome.'

'And a chocolate figure of the tyrant, perhaps?' suggested the Pastry Chef.

'Yes, yes,' said the Prince. 'Standing inside the palace walls. That will show that I believe Talbor to be the rightful ruler of Schwartzgarten.'

'Even if he isn't,' said Kalvitas.

'Exactly,' said Prince Eugene.

'I can make the chocolate figure of Talbor,' said Frederick.

'No, no,' said the Prince. 'That is a task for Kalvitas.'

Kalvitas bowed his head.

Frederick seethed and Elka smirked at him. The boy's hatred for Kalvitas grew and grew and he vowed to take his revenge.

———

In the days before Talbor's visit the palace kitchens hummed with activity. Flour was weighed, spices were pounded and sugar fondant was beaten and rolled so many times it became as white as mountain snow. Chocolate tortes were baked by the dozen to form the base of the edible palace and the soaring buttresses were stuffed with poached pears, piped full of vanilla cream and studded with slivered almonds. Slowly, piece by delicious piece, the palace took shape.

Kalvitas worked hard to make the figure of Talbor, with boots of dark chocolate and a face of caramel, but the more he thought of his encounters with the tyrant the stickier his hands became, so that the figure kept melting away between his fingers.

At night, when he could work unseen, Frederick also used his art to make another figure: a figure of Prince Eugene. Dark deeds were afoot.

———

On the day of Emeté Talbor's arrival at the Summer Palace, Kayakovsky and Bagelbof prepared the young prince. But it was hard work indeed.

'Do not bow too low,' warned Kayakovsky. 'It might be seen as a sign of weakness.'

'And do not blink too hard, Majesty,' said Bagelbof. 'He has cut off the noses of many men for less.'

'Don't do this, don't do that,' muttered the Prince. 'Is there anything I *can* do?'

Emeté Talbor's carriage thundered into the courtyard of the Summer Palace, followed by a regiment of soldiers on horseback. The door of the carriage swung open and

Emeté Talbor appeared from inside. The Imperial orchestra struck up and Talbor snarled them into silence. There was a gasp from the assembled courtiers – as if they had woken from a bad dream to find a monster standing before them. Prince Eugene's legs shook and his tongue was dry.

Talbor's long hair had been pulled back into a tight knot, and his dark eyes sparkled more malevolently than ever. Two footmen ran forward with steps, which they pushed into place beside the carriage. Talbor stepped down onto the cobbled courtyard and gave a low and elaborate bow. His spurs clicked as he approached Prince Eugene and Princess Euphenia.

'It is a pleasure to meet you,' said Prince Eugene, struggling to get the words from his lips and bowing low, but not too low, as he ushered his visitor into the palace.

Princess Euphenia giggled and curtsied and Talbor gave her the snarl that was the closest he ever came to a smile.

Volkoff had returned from Schwartzgarten with Talbor. He was impatient, waiting for his life to change. If war were to occur, he was determined to be the man to provoke it.

'I would like to visit the kitchens,' he said to Kayakovsky, taking the adviser to one side. 'To make quite sure that all is in order for the banquet.'

Kayakovsky nodded and led the Ambassador downstairs.

⚫

To amuse the tyrant, Princess Euphenia had arranged for Talbor to be shown the guillotine from the late Prince Alberto's antique collection of instruments of torture. A wax figure had been put in position to demonstrate the guillotine's workings.

'What a delicious entertainment,' said Emeté Talbor, tugging at a cord proffered by a palace footman. The blade dropped, the wax head was sliced cleanly from the neck and sawdust spilled out onto the floor. Emeté Talbor applauded. He pulled his sword from its scabbard and thrust the tip into the wax head, jerking it aloft. 'The effect would be more pleasing with a living victim. You!' He pointed to a young soldier in his entourage, and the unfortunate man took a faltering step forward. 'Place your head in there,' said Talbor, pointing to the guillotine.

'You want to see him beheaded?' gasped Prince Eugene.

'My powers of imagination are limited,' replied Emeté

Talbor with a smile that chilled Prince Eugene's blood. 'I can never tell how effective an instrument of destruction might be unless I see it for myself.' He clapped his hands impatiently.

Though Prince Eugene had been taught well not to contradict his visitor, this was too much for him. 'But we would need a basket,' he protested, desperately thinking up an excuse to prevent the guillotining and horrified at the thought of an un-basketed head rolling unpredictably across the floor, spurting blood in all directions. 'Without it, who can tell where the man's head might end up?'

Princess Euphenia clapped her hands in delight and Emeté Talbor gurgled with laughter.

'Like a game, then!' he exclaimed. 'I think the head will stop here!' He planted his boot firmly on the floor a good ten yards from the foot of the guillotine. 'Now,' he insisted, 'I want a proper demonstration.' He clicked his fingers. 'You, I have asked you once already and I will not be kept waiting.'

On shaking legs, the soldier took another step forward.

'Yes, yes,' whispered Princess Euphenia, her breath quickening with excitement.

'Perhaps he doesn't want to be beheaded,' suggested Prince Eugene.

'If he doesn't obey, then he knows there'll be a worse end for him when we return to Schwartzgarten,' replied Talbor.

The Prince stared at the man in disbelief. 'A worse end than *guillotining*?'

As the unwilling victim prepared to offer his neck to the blade the dinner gong echoed along the corridors of the palace.

'Dinner!' exclaimed Prince Eugene, much relieved.

'Unfortunate,' said Talbor with a grin. 'I was looking forward to a little blood-letting before we ate. It sharpens the appetite.'

The soldier's legs buckled and he slumped to the floor, quivering uncontrollably, while Talbor followed Princess Euphenia as she skipped towards the Banqueting Hall.

The tablecloth had been starched and smoothed; the edges were so stiff they could have cut like knife blades. Vines and ivy trailed around silver candlesticks that glittered in the pulsing candlelight.

All through dinner, Emeté Talbor discussed what might happen when his soldier's head was cleft from his shoulders by the polished blade of the guillotine, tipping red wine from his glass to illustrate the possible flow of blood. Princess Euphenia was entranced by their guest and laughed and clapped gleefully, all the time wishing that her husband the Prince was the sort of ruler who would call for soldiers to be beheaded whenever the mood took him.

Between courses, and at the Princess's insistence, Bagelbof presented Emeté Talbor with the original blueprints for the guillotine, so that he might construct his own instrument of death on his return to Schwartzgarten.

'Excellent, excellent!' exclaimed Talbor, slurping back an oyster and tossing the shell to the floor. He opened his mouth wide and produced a belch of such force that the table trembled. Prince Eugene, whose manners were superior, dabbed the corners of his mouth with his napkin, and delicately wiped his fingers. He was appalled by Talbor's habits but too polite and too scared to say so.

The floor was soon scattered with oyster shells and the Dowager Princess watched the guest with distaste.

'If my husband, the late Prince Alberto, had been alive to witness this,' she murmured to Volkoff in disbelief, 'he would have cut the man's head from his shoulders the moment he set foot through the palace gates.'

Emeté Talbor swallowed without chewing and Prince Eugene watched, open-mouthed.

'Are you still eating from our china?' asked the Dowager. 'The china you stole from us when you took the palace in Schwartzgarten?'

'Be quiet, Mother,' whispered Prince Eugene, a fixed smile on his face. 'We would not wish to offend our guest, would we?'

But Talbor was not listening. There was a trumpet fanfare and the doors to the Banqueting Hall swung open. The tyrant watched in fascination as the edible palace was carried in on a solid silver tray, borne on the shoulders of the palace pastry chefs. Kalvitas kept his head down, desperate that Talbor would not recognise him.

It was a magnificent dessert and the guests gasped in wonder. The high buttresses of the palace rose steeply from a base of sugar cobblestones. The tiles on the roof were carved from the darkest chocolate and the dome was formed from strands of spun caramel. The gargoyles leering from the corner of each wall were shaped from almond paste and the windowpanes were made of sugar-glass. Miniature cannons had been added, forged in the palace armoury, and though they could not be eaten they were designed to fire edible cannonballs of dried lingonberries dipped in egg white and rolled in powdered sugar.

'Observe!' cried Prince Eugene, lighting a taper and igniting one of the miniature cannons, then watching as the lingonberry cannonball soared through the air, landing in the wide-open mouth of Princess Euphenia, who clapped her hands more excitedly than ever. 'This dessert is to prove,' said Prince Eugene, 'that we can live in peace together. That you are the rightful' – the Prince blinked – 'that you are the *rightful* ruler of Schwartzgarten.'

Talbor grunted.

'Press the handle of the palace gates,' urged Prince Eugene.

Volkoff waited expectantly.

Emeté Talbor rose to his feet. With a frown of concentration, he pushed a small brass button on the gate and a clockwork mechanism rattled away inside the edible palace.

'Look!' cried Prince Eugene. 'See? The flag!'

But to the Prince's surprise, it was not a miniature of

the raven banner, but his own flag – the Imperial Standard with the symbol of the eagle – that rose above the caramel dome of the palace.

'What?' roared Emeté Talbor. 'What is this?'

'A mistake, a mistake!' insisted Prince Eugene, snapping the flag from the pole and hiding it behind his back.

Volkoff held his wine goblet to his lips to conceal a fast-spreading grin.

Talbor was peering hard at the chocolate figure in the courtyard of the palace.

'It is a figure of you,' said Prince Eugene. 'Made entirely from chocolate.' He peered over the walls of the edible palace and was shocked to discover that the figure was not of Talbor, but of himself.

Frederick was watching the unfolding events with satisfaction. Holding in his hand the chocolate figure of Talbor, he smiled slyly to himself. He would punish Kalvitas, no matter what it cost him to do so.

'Who made this?' demanded Talbor, lifting up the chocolate figure of Prince Eugene and crushing it between finger and thumb. Catching sight of the lurking figure of Kalvitas, he cried out, 'You!' He extended a bejewelled finger and beckoned the boy forward. 'Your face is known to me, I think.' He seized Kalvitas by the ear and the boy squirmed and wriggled. 'Yes, yes, I know you,' continued Talbor. 'Don't deny it, boy. The raven slayer. You think you can humiliate me? Emeté Talbor? You think this stupid, fat prince should rule over Schwartzgarten instead of me?' He gulped back his wine and slammed the goblet down on the table with such force that the sugar-glass panes cracked in the windows of the edible palace. He seized Kalvitas by the neck. 'Perhaps we will have a beheading after all.'

Prince Eugene opened his mouth to cry out, but it was was dry and no sound came. As Talbor prepared to drag Kalvitas from the room towards the waiting guillotine, the Pastry Chef stepped forward and pulled the boy close to him.

'You won't harm a hair on his head,' he growled defiantly.

Emeté Talbor stared at Prince Eugene, who stared back and blinked twice.

'No one mocks me,' hissed Talbor. 'This is an act of war.' He strode from the room, followed by his entourage.

Prince Eugene did not know what to say. He stood, mouth agape, trying to make sense of the events that had so quickly unfolded.

'Well,' said the Dowager Princess, taking a sip of wine, 'only *you* could start war over a dessert.'

War Is Declared

PRINCE EUGENE sat slumped in the attiring room of his Imperial bedchamber. He could not put his mind to anything, and a tray of Kalvitas's marzipan and chocolate eagles lay uneaten in their dish.

Kayakovsky entered hurriedly, bearing a small envelope on a silver salver. He was followed close behind by Bagelbof.

'Is it from Talbor?' asked Prince Eugene, sitting up suddenly.

'It bears his seal, Majesty,' replied Kayakovsky.

With a trembling hand, Prince Eugene reached out for the message. It was sealed with black wax and stamped with an image of a raven pecking at a skull. 'Maybe he has written to say that he has changed his mind? That he will not go to war against us?' He took a deep breath, broke the seal and tore open the envelope.

Bagelbof and Kayakovsky stood expectantly as Prince Eugene read the missive in silence.

'What does it say, Majesty?' ventured Bagelbof.

The Prince tried to speak, but it felt as though a crumb

of cake had become lodged in his throat and he could hardly swallow. He passed the envelope to Kayakovsky.

It was a simple message:

Your armies will die. And then you will die.

Talbor

'He doesn't waste his words,' said Bagelbof grimly, returning the message to the salver.

The Dowager Princess entered the room, without so much as a knock. 'Well?' she said. 'What news is there?'

'Talbor has declared war,' whispered the Prince. He turned to Bagelbof and his voice rose like fluting birdsong. 'But perhaps we can change the tyrant's mind? Send for Ambassador Volkoff! Despatch pastries from the palace kitchens! There must be something that can be done!'

'You're a whimpering coward,' said the Dowager Princess quietly. 'Better that you had died and not your father.'

——◆——

This is all well and good, and adds gravy to the meat of my

story. But what happened to Kalvitas after the royal banquet? Was he clapped in irons and dragged to the deepest, darkest dungeon cell? That did not happen, though well it might have done. What happened was this.

'Did you make the figure of the Prince?' demanded the Pastry Chef. 'Did you replace Talbor's raven flag with the standard of the Imperial Family?'

'No,' pleaded Kalvitas. 'The flag was made of cast-sugar, and I painted on the raven myself. I placed the chocolate figure of Talbor on the sugar-cobbles of the edible palace as soon as we'd carried it up from the kitchens. There was only me, you and—'

'Frederick!' cried the Pastry Chef.

Frederick approached slowly, his head hung low.

'Was it you, boy?' asked the Pastry Chef.

Frederick opened his fist to reveal a puddle of chocolate that had once been the figure of Emeté Talbor.

'But why?' asked Kalvitas.

'Because you are more of a son to my father than I have ever been,' said Frederick quietly. 'And because you like Elka.'

'Tell them it was me that did it,' said Kalvitas, turning

to the Pastry Chef. 'Prince Eugene won't lock me up. He's my friend. And besides, I'm the only one that can make the marzipan and chocolate pastries for him.'

'I thought better of you, Frederick,' said the Pastry Chef. He held out his hand. 'And the flag as well?'

Frederick raised his head. 'What flag?' he asked. 'It was just the figure I changed, not the flag.'

And there was something in Frederick's eyes that convinced the Pastry Chef that his son was speaking the truth.

If you are an intelligent child, and most are not, then you will have guessed that the flag had been switched by Ambassador Volkoff...

———

By now you may be wondering what had become of Emeté Talbor. Did he start out at once to prepare for war? No, he did not. If you do not like dark things, then stop reading now and come back to this book when your brain is sharper and your stomach is stronger.

Returning home to Schwartzgarten, Talbor had given instructions that the palace gymnasium should house a guillotine, constructed in haste, following the blueprints from the Summer Palace. He could not sleep that night, for his head was full of tantalising and delicious thoughts of the beheadings to come.

The effect was more spectacular than even Talbor had imagined. The cheeks of the decapitated head of his first victim (a soldier, whose only crime had been to groan with the effort of carrying the completed guillotine into the gymnasium) blushed and the eyes seemed to roll back into their sockets. Emeté Talbor laughed and applauded. There was a strange gurgling, whistling noise from inside the headless body.

'What is that?' demanded Talbor.

'The air escaping from the man's lungs,' replied Glattburg, polishing the silver tip of his nose with his coat sleeve.

Talbor gave the decapitated head a gentle tap with the toe of his boot, and watched as it rolled across the marble floor. 'Send for an artist!' cried the tyrant with a grin. 'I want a painting of the head to hang from the wall!'

Talbor looked for each and every chance to use his new guillotine. He sentenced men to death for being too tall, or too short, for being too greedy or not greedy enough. And he attended every execution, sitting in a throne at the foot of the guillotine to watch as the heads rolled across the floor. But as with all his instruments of death and torture, the novelty of the new guillotine soon began to wane. Even blunting the blade to slow down the beheading did little to increase Emeté Talbor's enjoyment. He ordered that the marble floor of the gymnasium be painted as a giant games board, with the words 'innocent' and 'guilty' marked inside large red circles. If the head of one of Talbor's victims landed on the word 'innocent', then the prisoner's family (waiting anxiously in the dungeons far beneath the palace) would be released. If, however, the head rolled forward onto the word 'guilty', then the prisoner's family met with an altogether less happy fate – they were executed with a second guillotine, which had enough holes for five victims to be beheaded at a single stroke.

Countless portraits of the decapitated heads, painted on Talbor's orders, soon hung in gilt frames and lined the walls of the gymnasium. Though times in Schwartzgarten were even deadlier than before, never had things been better for portrait artists with a talent for capturing the likeness of a severed head.

Ambassador Volkoff admired his reflection in the mirror-smooth blade of the guillotine. He had grown tired of Talbor's obsession with beheading, and was anxious that the tyrant should turn his thoughts to the more pressing matter of overthrowing Prince Eugene.

'Bagelbof informs me that the young prince has already raised a large army,' said Volkoff, though this was quite untrue. 'But if you carry on with your endless chopping you will have no soldiers left to fight him.'

'You might be up there one day,' grinned Emeté Talbor, gesturing to the walls behind him on which were now displayed the portraits of five hundred severed heads. 'I can behead ambassadors too, you know.'

Volkoff bowed. 'I trust that will never happen, Excellency,' he replied. 'There is no man in Schwartzgarten more loyal to you than I.'

He was a polished liar. He would be loyal to Talbor only as long as it suited him to do so.

In the Summer Palace, Prince Eugene had spent a peaceful

afternoon designing uniforms for his soldiers, trying desperately to put the grim matter of the coming war from his mind.

'No, no. Too plain,' sighed the Prince, examining a tunic on a tailor's mannequin. 'My soldiers must look elegant on the battlefield as they face the enemy.'

'What would you have me do, Majesty?' asked the Court Tailor.

'More gold, more gold,' said the Prince after a moment of thought.

Bagelbof and Kayakovsky entered and bowed.

'What news do you bring me?' asked Prince Eugene, as the Court Tailor added extra loops of gold braid to the uniform.

'What news were you expecting?' asked Kayakovsky politely.

The Prince gave a hopeless shrug.

'Emeté Talbor's army is massing,' said Bagelbof. 'The day of battle draws close. General Montelmarte will be at the palace by supper time to receive your orders, Majesty.'

'But how can I tell the man the way to lead an army?' wailed Prince Eugene. 'I am not a soldier like my father. I am a *poet*!'

Prince Alberto's heroism in battle was well documented, recorded in leather-bound books that lined the library shelves of the Summer Palace, vividly detailing the bloody skirmishes in which he had fought. At Bagelbof's suggestion, Prince Eugene now prepared to read the books in preparation for war, with Vincenzo to assist him.

Galfridus, the Court Librarian, struggled to the table with an armful of books. He was so heavily laden that he walked bow-legged as he piled countless volumes in front of Prince Eugene, who groaned in despair.

The Prince picked up a book at random.

THE BATTLES OF PRINCE ALBERTO: A HISTORY

Never was there a man more heroic than Brave Prince Alberto. Thrice he fought the Tyrant Emeté Talbor in three bloody battles outside the walls of the Great City of Schwartzgarten. Talbor was the Darkness and Crown Prince Alberto was the Light...

'Will I have to read very much?' asked Prince Eugene.

'It may prove instructive, Majesty,' replied Vincenzo.

'Are there many more books?' gasped the Prince as Galfridus placed another fat volume, bound in red calfskin, on the table in front of him.

'This is a most interesting tome, Majesty,' said Galfridus. 'It was your father's own book. He said you might have use of it one day. But as you can see, the clasp is locked and there is no key.'

Seized by a moment of inspiration, Prince Eugene reached into his pocket and pulled out the golden key that his father had given him on his death bed. He inserted the key in the lock and found that it turned easily. Whatever secret Prince Alberto had to tell his son would surely now be revealed. But the young Prince sighed when he turned the pages of the book and found that it contained nothing more than further descriptions of his father's battle exploits. Nothing more, that is, but a small slip of paper inside the back cover of the book, on which words had been written in the neat hand of Prince Alberto.

If you are reading this, Eugene, then I am dead in my grave. I will have told you of Gutterfink as I breathed my last, and you will now know my darkest truth. There are three reasons why you might seek this man out.

1) Gutterfink has broken his promise to me, in which case his head must be hacked from his neck, the treacherous rat.

2) You have reason to journey to Schwartzgarten, in which case the loyal Gutterfink holds the key.

3) Gutterfink has broken his promise but you also have reason to journey to Schwartzgarten, in which case you must hack off the man's head after taking the key, and not before. My brother Rufus alone can guide you to Gutterfink's hovel.

Prince Eugene turned to Galfridus, his eyes wide with surprise. 'So Gutterfink is a *person*.'

The librarian raised his eyebrows. 'Majesty?'

'Who is Gutterfink?'

But neither Galfridus nor Vincenzo could shed any light on the matter.

'Then I shall ask my Uncle Rufus,' said the Prince. 'Summon him at once.'

Vincenzo and Galfridus exchanged nervous glances.

'But Prince Rufus is dead, Majesty,' said Galfridus at last.

'The news has only arrived this very day, Majesty,' said Vincenzo.

'I'm always the last to know everything,' said Prince Eugene.

'Your uncle had been holidaying by the shores of Lake Taneva. It seems he died the very moment he heard word of your father's untimely death,' said Galfridus.

'They were always close,' said Prince Eugene. 'We are not a long-lived family.' Sighing, he folded the paper and slipped it inside his jacket pocket. He resolved to carry it with him wherever he went until the mystery could be uncovered.

With a yawn, he turned to the first page of Prince Alberto's book; it was as dull as any he had already read. He was fast growing bored with his father's military campaigns.

Although it was not a large book, it had been divided

into one hundred and seventeen chapters, each set out in such small and dense print that it was impossible to read the words without the aid of a magnifying glass.

Slowly Prince Eugene turned to the second chapter. And the more he read, the more it seemed that the words were swimming before him. They appeared to merge together in a solid mass, and his eyes began to flicker shut. He snorted himself awake and sat upright in his chair. He closed the book and from his pocket removed a copy of Constantin Esterburg's *The Virtue of the Violin*. Smiling, he opened the familiar volume and began to read.

Prince Eugene felt certain that he would never have to fight in battle. But we cannot tell where Fate will lead us when he extends his bony finger and beckons us on.

So the fat Prince wasted his time reading a book for pleasure when he would have been better occupied preparing for life as a soldier. Reader, let this be a lesson to you.

Generals are not unlike dominoes – once one is toppled the others often follow suit. Such was the case with Prince Eugene's Imperial Army, and I will now describe the unfortunate deaths of the Prince's generals, as related in my popular book *Some Military Leaders and their Tragic Ends*.

THE DEATH OF GENERAL MONTELMARTE

———◆◆◆———

General Montelmarte was the bravest of men and placed great stock in surprising the enemy. Calculating that Talbor's army was encamped on the far side of a vast forest, he prepared to lead his soldiers through the trees to attack.

'We must advance,' declared General Montelmarte, drawing his sword from its scabbard and slashing at the undergrowth. 'Onward, through the forest!'

'But the wolves,' stammered a loyal foot soldier. 'We'll be ripped to shreds in their vicious jaws.'

'Nonsense,' retorted the General. 'There are no wolves here.' And to prove his point he stepped out into a clearing, threw back his head and howled like a wolf. 'You see?' grinned the General, waving his sword merrily. 'Not a wolf to be found!'

But General Montelmarte's howl was soon answered by another, from deep in the forest.

Before he could turn to run, the wolves were upon him. There was nothing that the General's men could do to save the man, so they decided not to try. Instead, they climbed the trees and watched, until every last scrap of General Montelmarte had been snapped up and swallowed by the slavering beasts.

'I told the General,' said the loyal foot soldier, as he peered down through the branches. 'Ripped to shreds, I said. And I was right, wasn't I?'

THE DEATH OF GRAND DUKE MORTBURG

Grand Duke Mortburg was a man of enormous appetite. If he was heard to say that he was hungry enough to consume a mountain horse whole, it was not so much a figure of speech as a statement of fact. Horse steaks or horse stews, horse sausages or horse pies, nothing pleased him more than a four-hooved feast. And if, on the battlefield, his horse stumbled in a shell hole or bridled at the sound of gunfire, Grand Duke Mortburg made certain that the offending horse was served at dinner in the officers' tent. But it was the Grand Duke's love of horsemeat that proved to be his undoing. As he attempted to cross a river on horseback, his steed shook its head and pawed nervously at the swiftly running water.

'On, you wretched creature,' shouted the Grand Duke, pulling up the reins and digging his spurs hard against the horse's flanks. 'On, I say, or it will be the dinner table for you.'

Still the horse did not obey. It lowered its head and gulped back a mouthful of river water, thick with green bileweed.

So the horse shared the fate of its brothers and sisters. It was broiled in its own juices and served up for dinner.

'Excellent!' cried the Grand Duke. 'Let this serve as a reminder that a general is always master of his horse!'

But a horse has one advantage over its master and it is this – a horse may eat green bileweed but a man may not.

Having taken a single mouthful of the tainted horsemeat, Grand Duke Mortburg clutched at his *stomach in pain.*

'That doesn't feel so good,' he belched. 'I'll probably be dead by daybreak.'

And true to his word, by the morning the General was stone-cold dead. He was nothing if not reliable.

To the grooms in Grand Duke Mortburg's stables it seemed fitting that a horse had finally taken its revenge on the ever-hungry General.

THE DEATH OF GENERAL NOISETTE

General Noisette was a vain and foolish man. He was more concerned with his appearance than fighting wars, and wherever he travelled he made sure that he was accompanied by a portrait artist, a man of skill who could capture in oil paint the General's strong chin, his long and elegant nose and his perfectly-formed eyebrows. But General Noisette nursed a secret sorrow. From an early age his hair had begun to slip from his cranium, like the sea ebbing from the shore, and by the age of twenty-five his head was as bald and as smooth as a pebble. A wig was ordered and swiftly arrived, woven from the shaven hair of insane criminals in the great asylum of Blödtanhaüsen. It was a wonderful wig, a thing of joy to the General, and it most perfectly matched the colour of his shapely eyebrows. From that day forth, man and wig were seldom parted.

In the corridors of the Summer Palace, gravity was enough to keep the wig in place, but on the field of battle a greater power was needed to hold the hair firmly in position. So the General ordered two crates of toupée glue, the strongest that money could buy, which were carried on horseback as he set off for war.

As battle raged around him, General Noisette posed for the portrait artist, with one hand upon the hilt of his sword and the other hand gesturing to the beautiful locks of hair that he had so lovingly glued to his head.

But alas, as the painter daubed at his canvas, a rocket whistled high above the battlefield and sparks rained down upon the head of the vain General. The wig ignited in an instant, setting fire to the toupée glue beneath, which flared brightly in a haze of purple vapour.

Though the General fought to pull the blazing wig from his head, the glue was so strong that no amount of tugging would release it. Backwards and forwards he ran, burning brilliantly like a human firework. He moved so quickly that it was difficult for the artist to paint him.

In a matter of moments, the General had burned quite completely – from the top of his head to the tips of his toes.

The final portrait of General Noisette still hangs in the Governor's Palace, and will be known to many of my readers. It is entitled: 'GOLDEN SUNSET'.

THE DEATH OF GENERAL BRATISLAV

General Bratislav was an ingenious man who had invented many hundreds of intriguing ways to kill and maim the enemy. He was the smallest of the generals in Prince Eugene's army and was called 'sparrow' by his soldiers, though never to his face.

'I have designed a new weapon,' announced General Bratislav one fine afternoon as an enormous iron cannon was wheeled out onto the battlefield. 'One blast alone is enough to slaughter an entire battalion.'

The little general climbed a ladder to squint through the telescopic sights as a soldier loaded the charge of gunpowder and rolled a mighty lead cannonball into the barrel of the gargantuan gun.

'Fire!' ordered the General.

The soldier lit the fuse, which crackled and hissed, but the cannon would not fire.

'Most, most inconvenient,' twittered General Bratislav, and gave orders that the field cannon should be cleaned and greased with hog fat.

Once again the weapon was charged and stoked, before the cannonball was rolled into place.

'Fire!' cried General Bratislav once more.

The soldier lit the fuse, but no burst of gunpowder issued forth. 'It will not fire, General,' said the soldier apologetically.

'Will not fire?' repeated General Bratislav, jumping on the spot and waving his arms, which seemed to flap and flutter like tiny wings. 'I designed the cannon, you fool! Of course it will fire!'

The General craned his head inside the cannon just as the powder was finally and fatally ignited. There was a bright flash of light and a violent explosion rocked the ground.

'See the sparrow fly!' cried a soldier nearby, as the General's head was blown from the cannon, arcing high above the battlefield before disappearing from sight.

General Bratislav's body was buried beneath the spot on which it fell. His head was discovered thirty miles beyond the battlefield, where it had landed in the chimneypot of a baker's shop, like an egg in an egg cup.

A General Of Wood
And Metal

W AR IS a nasty business and there are few rules. But one thing that is known by even the simplest-minded fool is this – the army that kills most men is the army that will return from the battlefields victorious.

For Prince Eugene's army, matters had gone from bad to worse to unimaginably awful. The soldiers of the Imperial Army were dying by the score, and to replace them, farmers and shopkeepers and old men from the town below the Summer Palace were being transported by train to face Talbor and the Dark Count.

At night, the skies above the Summer Palace burned bright as the sulphurous furnaces of the Imperial Mint struggled to keep up with the endless demand for medallions, to commemorate the untimely deaths of Prince Eugene's generals. And, though she protested, the lead from the Dowager Princess's collection of death masks was melted down so that more medallions could be struck.

'You're certain they are not dying deliberately?' asked the Prince, sitting down to breakfast one grey morning.

'It is a tragedy indeed,' said Kayakovsky sadly. 'To lose so many generals and so quickly too.'

'I never liked General Bratislav,' said the Dowager Princess and took a spoonful of her boiled egg. 'Men should be like bears, not birds.'

'What do you think, my dear?' asked the Prince, turning to Princess Euphenia. 'Who should lead my troops now?'

But the Princess did not speak a word. She chewed rhythmically on a slice of toast, daydreaming of coffins and corpses.

'There is General Falkenstein,' suggested Kayakovsky. 'A very wise general and an excellent leader of men.'

Prince Eugene turned brightly. 'Then appoint him,' he cried. 'What are you waiting for?'

'The man is dead,' interrupted Bagelbof. 'I received word of it this very morning.'

Kayakovsky stared in surprise. 'Dead?'

'The general was sliced in half by his own sword,' replied Bagelbof. 'It fell from the luggage rack as he arrived by train at the battlefield.'

'Are any of my generals still alive?' squealed the Prince.

'What news is there of Marshal Pfefferberg?' asked Kayakovsky.

'The man has disappeared,' said Bagelbof. 'No word has been heard from him in weeks.'

The Dowager Princess snorted as she scraped up the last of her egg. 'Either he is too afraid or too dead to be of help.'

'Too dead,' echoed Princess Euphenia dreamily.

We have met Marshal Maurice Pfefferberg already in this history of Prince Eugene, though fleetingly. If you chanced to blink your eyes you would have missed him. In his day the Marshal was a fighting man without equal. Sitting upon his steed, a chestnut stallion known fondly as Gallant, he had been the pride of Prince Alberto's army. Never before has a soldier been more skilful with the blade – he was so swift and so neat with his sword that it was sometimes said that his vanquished enemies would run about for a day or more without realising that their heads had been sliced from their shoulders. But that was in the past. Marshal Pfefferberg had disappeared the very day war was declared and he showed little sign of reappearing.

Kayakovsky was fast running out of ideas. 'What about Grand Duke Sergei?' he ventured after a long pause. 'He is a highly-decorated general.'

'But all his men were killed, weren't they?' whispered the Prince. 'What was he decorated for?'

'For surviving, Majesty,' said Bagelbof.

Grand Duke Sergei arrived at the Summer Palace the next morning. He was so ancient that it took him very nearly five minutes to cross the Grand Hall. The military decorations he wore round his neck were so weighty that he walked with a stoop, leaning heavily on his walking stick.

'You are very welcome, Grand Duke Sergei,' said Prince Eugene, as the General finally approached the Imperial throne.

Grand Duke Sergei held up an ear trumpet. 'What's that you say?' he asked.

'You are very welcome,' repeated Prince Eugene.

'Eh?' said Grand Duke Sergei.

'YOU...HAVE BEEN...A GENERAL...A GREAT MANY YEARS,' shouted Prince Eugene.

Grand Duke Sergei nodded. 'I knew your father when he was as tall as this...' He bent down to indicate the height of the infant Prince Alberto, only to find that he could not get up again. 'I'm not as young as I once was,' he explained as Kayakovsky helped him into a chair. 'My leg, for example...' He struck his leg with the walking stick; it gave a dull metallic echo. 'Hollow, see? And my right hand is silver, a gift from your father. The only bits of me that are any good are made of wood and metal.'

'Even his brain is made of wood,' murmured Bagelbof, and was silenced by a frown from Prince Eugene.

'Eh?' said Grand Duke Sergei. 'What was that?'

'Bagelbof says that we need you to lead our army into battle,' said the Prince quickly.

'Need me to do what?' asked Grand Duke Sergei.

'LEAD...OUR...ARMY...INTO...BATTLE...' screamed the Prince.

'Battle,' chuckled Grand Duke Sergei, climbing to his feet and saluting. 'Then I must pack at once.'

Kayakovsky stooped to retrieve the Grand Duke's silver hand, which had dropped with a loud clank from the sleeve of the old man's tunic.

The Grand Duke received his right hand gratefully and saluted with the left. Slowly he retreated – so slowly that Prince Eugene was almost asleep by the time the man finally turned the doorknob and stepped from the room. With a final salute as the doors were closed, Grand Duke Sergei disappeared from view.

'And you think he's the best chance of leading us to victory against Emeté Talbor?' said Prince Eugene brokenly. 'He'll probably be dead within a week.'

There was an urgent knock at the door and a courtier entered.

'Terrible news, Majesty.'

'Yes, yes?' said the Prince. 'What is it now?'

'It's Grand Duke Sergei,' said the courtier.

'Well?' sighed Prince Eugene. 'What about him?'

'He's dead, Majesty,' continued the courtier.

'Dead?' gasped Prince Eugene, rising from his throne. 'But he can't be dead! Was it one of Talbor's men? Was there an assassin lurking behind the door?'

'No, Majesty,' replied the courtier, with a respectful bow of his head. 'It seems it was the strain of turning the doorknob.'

Maximus

T HE OBSERVANT reader will have noticed that Prince Eugene's uncle, the Archduke, has been absent from this story for some time. Furthermore, it may seem surprising that a man raised from birth on a diet of gunshot and gunpowder should have missed an opportunity to gallop into the fray and shoot with his pistol and slice with his sword.

It had simply not come to the Archduke's attention that war had been declared, occupied as he was on an expedition to hunt wild bears. But arriving back at his castle in the north and discovering with delight that battle was in progress, he sent a telegram at once to Prince Eugene:

```
So all your generals are dead STOP It is time
you became a soldier STOP I shall set off by
carriage tonight STOP
```

Returning to the Summer Palace to prepare the young

prince for war, the Archduke was aghast to discover his nephew seated at a table in the library with a dish of honey pastries, reading to Vincenzo from his newly-published book: *The Correct Way to Peel and Core a Pear.*

'You have the proud blood of the Imperial Family coursing through your veins,' erupted the Archduke, picking up the volume and flinging it across the room. 'And yet you waste your time writing books!'

'I write because I enjoy writing,' stammered the Prince. 'And it is important to instruct people to be civilised when eating.'

'Any other fruit, or just pears?' enquired the Archduke sarcastically.

'My next book will discuss the best way of eating an orange without dribbling juice,' said the Prince. 'It is a problem that afflicts many people.'

'You should have taught your charge to become a soldier,' said the Archduke, holding his monocle to his eye so he could glare more ferociously at Vincenzo. 'But instead he is a writer of books on *fruit.*'

'The prince is a poet as well, sir,' protested Vincenzo.

'Even worse!' screamed the Archduke, and gave orders

that the Tutor should be banished from the palace, never to return.

The next morning, before breakfast, the Archduke began training his nephew for war.

Prince Eugene was given a sword, as a groom hung a sack of grain from an iron hook at the far end of the stable yard.

'Now, charge!' bellowed the Archduke.

Prince Eugene obeyed his uncle's orders and lunged at the sack with his sword, only to slip on the cobbles and fall headlong into a steaming mound of horse dung. He staggered to his feet.

'Now cut at him with your sword!' screamed the Archduke.

The Prince stabbed desperately at the sack, which swung forward on its hook, striking him heavily in the stomach and knocking him backwards onto his rump.

'If you can be defeated so easily by a sack of grain with no arms or legs then I would rather serve under the sack,' growled the Archduke, leaving Prince

Eugene sprawled on the ground.

'But, Uncle,' pleaded the unfortunate Prince. 'I can learn. I can improve. I know I can. I need time, that's all.'

'Your mother told me you were a hopeless lump and I doubted her word,' said the Archduke, turning back to face his nephew. 'I would have done well to listen.'

He made his way in to breakfast as his nephew trudged miserably back to the palace to wash, after which Prince Eugene was dressed in his military uniform, his highly polished black boots glimmering like beetles. His tunic was peacock blue, lined in silk, with a trim of silver and gold brocade. A large gold star had been embroidered on the breast of the tunic and his hat was adorned with grey-and-brown-striped osprey feathers. Prince Eugene peered at his reflection in the mirror. It was a beautiful uniform and it cheered his spirits.

When the Prince came down to breakfast, the Archduke was already seated at the table, helping himself to a third veal steak.

'And a cup of the blackest, strongest coffee the kitchens have ever brewed,' he barked, hurling a bread roll at a passing footman.

'And I will have hot chocolate with cinnamon, and a froth of cream,' added the Prince, sitting at the table and heaping his plate with custard pastries.

The Archduke roared like a caged beast and flung the Prince's plate from the table. 'You will eat veal, like a real soldier! And you will drink coffee! Pastries and chocolate are not the foods of a fighting man.'

'The Prince has become an excellent military tactician,' volunteered Kayakovsky, who was looming uncertainly. 'Most encouraging, most encouraging.'

But the Archduke only grunted.

The Dowager Princess swept into the breakfast room and fixed Prince Eugene with her gaze. 'You haven't shaved,' she said.

'I am growing a moustache, Mother,' said the Prince obstinately.

'It becomes you,' said the Dowager Princess.

'Thank you, Mother,' replied the Prince, hardly able to believe such a compliment.

'It helps to hide your fat face,' continued the Dowager Princess.

Prince Eugene took a sip of his coffee and pretended not

to have heard. 'I think Father might have been proud of me, after all,' he murmured. 'To see me dressed for battle.'

The Dowager Princess stared hard at her son, her eyes more wolf-like than ever. 'It would take more than polished boots and a plume of osprey feathers to convince your father that you had amounted to more than a hopeless mound of flesh. It's one thing for a man to wear a uniform, quite another for him to live up to it.'

'Yes, Mother,' said Prince Eugene, slicing petulantly into his veal steak.

After breakfast, the Archduke tried once more to prepare Prince Eugene for war. From the palace stables he had selected a purebred stallion as the Prince's battle steed. It was a beast that would strike fear into the hearts of the enemy, of that the Archduke was quite certain, and it responded to the name of Maximus.

'There you are at last,' bellowed the Archduke as Prince Eugene made his way gingerly towards the stables. 'About time.'

'Will it be a very large horse?' enquired Prince Eugene.

The Archduke glared grimly at his nephew. 'Afraid of horses?' he snorted. 'No prince is afraid of horses!' He called out to a passing groom. 'Bring Maximus to me!'

Maximus was led across the courtyard. He was a large, black stallion, with a blaze of white that ran the length of his muzzle. The horse snorted, filling the air with hot breath, and Prince Eugene backed away.

'This,' said the Archduke, 'is a horse. Stop me if I'm going too quickly for you.'

'You are not,' answered Prince Eugene.

'You feed this end,' barked the Archduke, gesturing to the horse's snarling mouth, then pointed to the horse's rump with his stick. 'You clean up at that end. And that is as much as a prince ever needs to know. Now climb up into the saddle.'

Prince Eugene did as he was told, helped into position by the groom. He grasped the reins tightly. The horse snorted but did not move. Prince Eugene settled back into the saddle and smiled nervously. 'Perhaps Maximus is a gentle-natured horse, after all,' he murmured.

'A horse without a temper is fit only for the glue factory,' said the Archduke, slapping Maximus hard on the flank.

The horse whinnied and rose up in anger, jerking his head so violently that he wrenched the reins from the hands of the waiting groom.

'Dig your spurs in!' screamed the Archduke. 'Show the horse that you're master!'

But though the Prince tried to control the creature, it seemed that Maximus had other ideas. Galloping in a circle around the stable courtyard the horse bucked and twisted, trying every trick to throw Prince Eugene from the saddle. The harder the Prince yanked at the reins the more desperately Maximus tried to fling him to the ground. His osprey feather hat tumbled from his head and was trampled underfoot. It was only when the groom tipped oats and barley into a trough that the horse came to a halt and Prince Eugene was helped from the saddle by five footmen. His legs were trembling so violently that he could not stand and had to be carried back into the palace.

That afternoon, the courtiers of the Imperial palace gathered in the attiring room to make offerings of the gifts Prince Eugene would carry with him to battle. There was a golden snuffbox, which played Princess Euphenia's favourite song, *Death Comes A-Waltzing*, whenever he lifted the lid. There was a pocket telescope of red jasper, mounted in gold and set with diamonds and rubies, and a toilette box of beaten gold which contained:

- A pocket almanac, with leather covers and clasps of silver (so that the Prince might record his exploits in battle)
- A tongue-scraper (to keep the Prince's tongue pink and healthy)
- An ear-pick (to scrape wax from the Prince's ears) and a golden flask (to collect the royal earwax)
- A miniature golden lance (to pierce the Prince's pimples), a pair of golden pincers (to squeeze out the pimple juices that were contained within and a second golden flask (to contain the said pimple juices)
- A fork (for eating, or for stabbing the enemy if not eating)
- Assorted spoons of silver and polished horn (for dessert, or to administer poison to enemy soldiers)

- A silver salt pot (to give flavour to bland food or to throw in the face of the approaching enemy)
- A toothpick (to occupy the Prince when not fighting)
- Combs (to groom the Prince's flourishing moustache and any other facial hair that threatened to erupt)
- A silver button hook with an ebony handle (to fasten the Prince's boots – or to stab the enemy)
- Eleven clothes brushes of different sizes (to protect the Prince's uniform or to hurl at the enemy if all else failed)

Finally, the Prince was armed with a helmet, a pair of jewelled gauntlets, and a battle sword and sheath. The sword was forged of steel, embellished with gold, and set with many hundreds of diamonds and emeralds.

Prince Eugene's mouth had gone dry. 'Will I have much use of a sword?' he clacked. 'Or is it mostly to impress the enemy?'

'It is to cut down the enemy in battle, Majesty,' said Kayakovsky.

Prince Eugene took a deep breath. 'And is it sharp?'

Kaspar, the Imperial Jeweller, bowed his head with modesty and professional pride. 'It would be quite impossible to make it any sharper, Majesty,' he observed, removing the blade from its sheath. He smiled and his teeth glittered with gold. 'You could slice off a man's arm with a single stroke.'

'As sharp as that?' said Prince Eugene, with a shudder that made his teeth rattle. 'Excellent, excellent.' He attempted a smile, though his blood ran cold.

'You flatter me, Majesty,' said Kaspar, with another bow of his head.

'Of course, Emeté Talbor is quite, quite insane,' observed Bagelbof, staring out of the window onto the courtyard below, where a battalion of the Prince's men were preparing to leave on horseback through the palace gates.

'And this will make it easier to defeat him, will it?' asked the Prince hopefully.

'Oh no, Majesty,' said Kayakovsky. 'Emeté Talbor will stop at nothing to destroy you. Unfortunately, madmen are often successful in such a task. Though it pains me to say so.'

Bagelbof nodded in agreement.

Prince Eugene dismissed his advisors with a wave of his hand, and hurried along the corridors of the palace to his private chambers. There he discovered Princess Euphenia, gazing into her mirror and sobbing.

'Don't cry,' said the Prince gently, touched to discover that at last his Princess was revealing her love for him. 'I will return safely to you, I promise.'

The Princess turned from the mirror. 'Haven't you left for the battlefields yet?' she demanded, her eyes dry as bone.

'I thought you were in distress, my sweet,' said Prince Eugene tenderly.

Princess Euphenia gave a laugh like fingernails on slate and shook her head.

'But you were sobbing,' said Prince Eugene.

'I was practising,' replied the Princess.

'For what, my darling?' asked the Prince.

Princess Euphenia gave a stomach-churning smile. 'For your death, of course,' she whispered.

The Prince let out a moan.

'But do not be concerned for me,' continued the Princess. 'I shall try not to think of all the horrible ways you might be killed – the bombs and the bullets, and the red-hot embers.'

She held out a small box to the Prince.

'For me?' he asked hoarsely.

The Princess smiled and nodded. The box contained a beautiful silver ring with the crest of the Imperial Family. 'Now open the ring,' she insisted. 'Open!'

Prince Eugene lifted the silver crest, to reveal a small cavity within. Nestling inside was a tiny, white pill.

'And what is that?' asked the Prince.

'Poison,' said Princess Euphenia. 'It is my gift to you.'

She picked up a needle and thread and continued work on an embroidered corpse-cloth for her coffin collection. She sang softly to herself as Prince Eugene stepped from the room. It did not calm his fears to discover that his wife was already making plans for his imminent death.

Outside, in the courtyard of the palace, bags and barrels were being loaded onto waiting wagons. Prince Eugene climbed timidly into the saddle of his horse (with eight grooms to steady the snorting, whinnying beast) and the Archduke, already mounted on his own steed, led him out through the palace gates. Bagelbof saluted the Prince and nodded his head approvingly. He was to remain at the palace, to take care of matters of state in Prince Eugene's absence.

The Prince battled to stay in the saddle as Maximus negotiated his way down the steep cobbled street from the palace. Flags and banners hung from the windows of shops and houses and the people cheered as the Prince passed by.

A small railway station with tall chimneys stood beside the river and the Stationmaster greeted Prince Eugene warmly.

'Battle is it, Majesty?' he grinned, his side whiskers bristling. 'How I wish I was thirty years younger and could cut down the enemy myself. The tales I'd have to tell!'

Prince Eugene smiled weakly. Had the Stationmaster been thirty years younger, he would have happily let the man take his place in battle. But the Stationmaster was old and that was that.

A coal fire burned in the waiting room and Prince Eugene warmed his hands as a goods train was loaded with supplies from the palace and Maximus and the Archduke's steeds were led up into their horse boxes. Prince Eugene peered miserably from the window as the goods train pulled out of the station. The Archduke stared grimly at his nephew as the mantel clock chimed the hour of four.

With a clattering of hooves, the Dowager Princess's horse-drawn carriage drew up outside the waiting room. The Dowager stepped down, accompanied by Monette and Ambassador Volkoff. She was muffled against the cold, and her face was as white as porcelain.

'Mother,' said Prince Eugene, 'it was so good of you to come!'

The Dowager Princess regarded her son with indifference but said nothing.

'Mother,' whispered the Prince. 'Tell me you wish me good fortune in battle.'

'Why would I tell you that?' asked the Dowager, staring quizzically at her son.

'Because you are my mother, Mother,' said the Prince. 'And I am your son.'

'What a curious thing to say,' said the Dowager, observing her son like an insect under the microscope. 'I came because I wanted to make quite certain that you didn't run away like the coward you are.' And without uttering another word, she turned her back on the Prince and swept noiselessly from the waiting room.

Ambassador Volkoff bowed stiffly at the waist. 'Do

not fear, Majesty,' he said. 'I shall take especial care of your wife and your mother. And if the unthinkable should happen and you do not return to us—'

Prince Eugene gave a croak of dismay and his lower lip trembled.

Volkoff bowed again. He clicked his heels together and hurried out to the Dowager's carriage to return to the Summer Palace.

With a hiss of steam, a gleaming railway engine, decorated with the brightly painted brass shields of the Imperial Family, slowly ground to a halt outside the station. Two footmen unrolled a red carpet from the waiting room to the Prince's Imperial railway carriage and the town band struck up as Prince Eugene and the Archduke prepared to board the train for the two-day journey to the battlefield.

The curious reader may wonder why Emeté Talbor had not sent his soldiers to attack the Summer Palace. But this was not a battle for land but a war of supremacy, and Talbor and the Dark Count were content for the two armies to engage in combat many hundreds of kilometres away from Schwartzgarten and the Summer Palace – at a place beyond the vast forests of the region, where Prince

Eugene's soldiers could more easily be defeated.

It was not the Prince and the Archduke alone that were to travel to the field of battle. Kayakovsky, the Court Physician, and the Prince's valet occupied another carriage and at the back of the train came the Imperial dining car.

A crowd had assembled on the platform. There were old men, and plump women with children, all waving flags and cheering as the Prince gave a half-hearted salute and climbed up into the carriage.

Kalvitas, who had run down the hill from the palace, pressed his way through the throng, but was pushed back by the Master-at-Arms.

'You can't come through,' barked the man. 'The train is ready to leave.'

'But I must see the Prince,' pleaded Kalvitas. 'I have a gift for him.'

'Gifts for princes?' laughed the Master-at-Arms. 'Get back before I have you dragged back.'

Kayakovsky was busy overseeing the Prince's portmanteau and cosmological clock as they were loaded onto the train. As the man passed by, Kalvitas called out to him.

'Chocolates!' he cried. 'For the Prince.'

Kayakovsky turned and, recognising Kalvitas, smiled.

Kalvitas pressed a small velvet casket into the man's hands and Kayakovsky nodded.

Sitting down in the Imperial carriage, Prince Eugene called out for his valet. 'A tray of chocolate and marzipan eagles from the dining car!'

'It's not a wonder that you're *fat*,' grunted the Archduke disdainfully. 'It's just a wonder that you're not *fatter*.'

The train slowly pulled away from the station and the chandelier rattled above Prince Eugene's head. He felt his stomach lurch.

'What will happen to me if I fail in battle?' he asked, choking back the lump in his throat.

'Then I expect you will be assassinated,' said the Archduke, staring distractedly out of the window at a passing horse. 'That's what usually happens.'

The Dowager Princess returned to the Summer Palace with Ambassador Volkoff. At last her son was gone, and unlikely to return.

'But what about Princess Euphenia?' asked Volkoff, as he climbed the stone steps to the Dowager Princess's tower. 'Do you think she will pine away and die, now that the Prince has gone?'

'With a little encouragement,' replied the Dowager Princess.

Volkoff smiled to himself, and in his head neatly crossed another name from the Imperial Family tree.

But Princess Euphenia had no intention of pining away and dying. Sitting alone in her room, she sipped from a cup of nettle tea, consumed by dark thoughts. Death was in her blood. She daydreamed of elaborate funeral processions. She was certain that a dead husband would be preferable to a living one.

The Princess drew endless sketches of Prince Eugene in his coffin, pulled in a glass hearse by black-plumed horses and escorted by a guard of honour. She even asked Constantin Esterberg to compose a Funeral March, in preparation for the glorious day when the Prince's ashen corpse might be carried home from the battlefields.

Many miles north of the Summer Palace, as the iron tracks crossed vast stretches of flat pastureland, the Imperial railway engine ground to a halt. Prince Eugene, who had been rocked to sleep by the swaying motion of his private carriage, climbed unsteadily to his feet.

'What is happening?' he called. 'Why have we stopped?' He opened the carriage door, which led through a narrow corridor to the dining car.

There stood the Archduke, shouting orders at two cowering stewards. 'Uncouple it, I said. We have no further need for the Imperial dining car.'

'Excuse me,' murmured Prince Eugene, and the Archduke swung round to face him.

'Yes?' he grunted.

Prince Eugene gave an apologetic cough and blinked. 'I must have misunderstood you, Uncle,' he said. 'My head is still fogged from sleep. But I thought I heard you shouting that the dining car was to be uncoupled?'

'Whatever's wrong with the rest of you, there's clearly nothing the matter with your hearing,' barked back the Archduke.

'But why, Uncle?' whined the Prince.

'Because you are too fat,' answered the Archduke. 'Because if you eat another mouthful of cake, you may very well explode. And if you're going to explode anywhere, then I want it to be on the battlefield!'

Prince Eugene could only watch in horror as the stewards uncoupled the dining car. His eyes misted over as the engine started up once more and the carriage receded slowly into the distance. The sugary scent of cakes and pastries lingered in the air and was then no more.

That evening, Prince Eugene sat at his desk as the carriage rattled and bumped along the railway tracks. He began to compose a letter to Princess Euphenia, to occupy his mind.

My dearest Euphenia...

His pen hovered in mid-air as he stared hard at the words. He shook his head, crumpled up the paper and handed it to Kayakovsky, who obediently dropped it into the wastepaper basket. Prince Eugene began the letter again on a fresh sheet of paper.

Prince Eugene sighed to himself. Though his wife did not love him, at least she did not hate him as much as his mother. 'After all,' he reasoned, 'she did care enough to give me poison.'

And as he pondered this unhappy thought an explosion rocked the carriage and the chandelier quivered. Prince Eugene spilled ink across his desk, which Kayakovsky attempted to mop up with a sheet of blotting paper.

The door swung open and the Archduke strode into the Imperial saloon. 'We have arrived!' he exclaimed with a smile that churned the contents of Prince Eugene's stomach. 'Kayakovsky, prepare the Prince for the battlefield!'

The Field Of Battle

$\bullet\!\!-\!\!\ast\!\!\ast\!\!\ast\!\!-\!\!\bullet$

DRESSED WARMLY in fur coat and hat, Prince Eugene was helped down from the Imperial carriage by two waiting infantrymen. As his polished boots sank slowly into the mud, he took in the flat landscape before him. It was a desolate view and his heart sank too. The nearby river had burst its banks and bled across the marshy land, the water reeking of rusting metal and rotten fish.

Kayakovsky gazed into the sky above. The clouds were quickly gathering and the horizon glowed orange from distant cannon fire.

'An ill-omened sky,' he whispered.

Beyond the railway halt stood an encampment of canvas tents, sheltered by the nearby forest – with a small kitchen and makeshift barracks for the troops. Prince Eugene shuddered as he saw Maximus snapping at a soldier in the stable tent.

Rain fell in a fine mist and the smell of gunpowder

hung heavily in the air.

'Breathe that in,' barked the Archduke, sniffing hard. 'Let it fill your lungs. That, my boy, is the scent of battle.'

The infantry stood to attention and saluted as Prince Eugene carried out an inspection of his troops. They were more rabble than army and the Prince saluted gloomily, his heart fluttering in his chest and his legs trembling in his boots.

Kayakovsky followed obediently as Prince Eugene made his way into his own tent. The Prince shook himself, as if the rain had sunk into his very bones and he was trying to rid himself of the penetrating damp. He glanced about him. For a prince, it was a sparsely furnished tent. There was a small campaign desk of polished rosewood, and a tall mahogany chest standing against the canvas wall. A map had been carefully set out on the desk, with wooden soldiers and horses in red to indicate Prince Eugene's army, and in black to indicate that of Emeté Talbor.

'What is this?' asked Prince Eugene.

'It is important that we should discuss military tactics,' said Kayakovsky.

'Can't we eat instead?' moaned the Prince. No sooner

had he spoken than an enormous blast rocked the ground beneath his feet. 'What was *that*?' he asked, cowering beneath his campaign desk.

'A mortar,' said Kayakovsky.

'And what is a mortar?' asked the Prince.

'In simple terms?' enquired Kayakovsky.

'As simple as you can make it,' hissed Prince Eugene, glaring up at the man as he crawled out from under the desk.

'A mortar, Majesty,' said Kayakovsky, 'is an explosive device—'

Prince Eugene interrupted. 'You mean a bomb?' he snapped.

Kayakovsky nodded. 'Yes, Majesty,' he replied. 'A bomb.'

The Archduke swept into the tent, eating pickled beetroot from a tin. 'Settling in, eh?' he barked. 'Ready for battle tomorrow, eh? Nothing like it to make a man out of a boy.'

'And where will you sleep?' asked Prince Eugene quietly, observing that there was only one bed in the tent and fearing that he would have to share it with his uncle.

'I will sleep with the troops,' replied the Archduke.

It was the first piece of good news the Prince had received since his arrival.

The daylight was failing fast, and as the Archduke made his way back outside to join his men, the Prince's valet lit a lantern and hung it from a hook in the ceiling of the tent.

'Go now, Kayakovsky,' said Prince Eugene to his advisor, 'and return when I am prepared for sleep.'

Kayakovsky bowed and stepped outside as the valet unpacked the Prince's portmanteau.

'War is not good for the skin,' observed Prince Eugene, gazing at his reflection in his pocket mirror and discovering a white-headed pimple that had appeared above his left eyebrow. He sighed as the valet squeezed at the spot with the pair of pincers from his toilette box and scraped the contents into the golden flask.

The Prince was dressed in his silk pyjamas, and attempted to make himself comfortable in the camp bed, propped up against a pile of furs. He sipped from the cup of hot chocolate that the valet had prepared – it was thick and grainy and tasted of soap. Oh, how the Prince missed Kalvitas.

There was a far-off roar of cannon fire.

'How can I sleep like this?' demanded Prince Eugene, pulling a pillow over his head as Kayakovsky returned. 'Can the cannons not be made less noisy?'

Kayakovsky smiled kindly at the Prince. He wound the mechanism of the brass cosmological clock and placed it on the mahogany chest beside the Prince's bed. 'Perhaps this will take your thoughts from battle, Majesty,' he said.

Prince Eugene watched as the earth slowly revolved around the golden sphere of the sun.

'Goodnight, Majesty,' said Kayakovsky, as the young prince settled down in bed.

———————

Prince Eugene slept fitfully. At six o'clock in the morning he was awakened by a mortar as it exploded high above the battlefield.

'Get up at once!' bellowed the Archduke, pulling back the canvas door to the tent.

'But it's barely dawn,' protested Prince Eugene, raising his head from the pillow.

'Yes,' snapped the Archduke. 'You've overslept.'

Prince Eugene's stomach ached and his head was swimming from lack of food. He was served a cup of strong black coffee and a bowl of cold goulash. 'The coffee is thicker than the food,' he complained, scraping away the grey scum that had formed on the surface of the goulash. 'This is hardly enough food to keep a rat alive. Bring me something else. Something better.'

'There is no more to eat, Majesty,' said the valet apologetically. 'Food is rationed on the Archduke's orders.'

Kayakovsky arrived, coughing politely but loudly to be heard above a distant explosion. 'A letter from the palace, Majesty,' he said, as he passed the envelope on a silver plate. It had been addressed in Princess Euphenia's distinctive writing, every i dotted with a hand-drawn skull. Prince Eugene sighed and unfolded the letter.

Have you been killed or injured yet, my brave Eugene? As I sit in the Summer Palace, sewing clothes for my little china corpses, I cannot help but wonder what terrible things have befallen you on the field of battle.

She had helpfully included illustrations of the terrible things she had in mind, with spurts of blood carefully drawn in with red ink.

And as I sit at dinner, feasting on macaroons and chocolate tortes, I think how cruel life is to deprive you of the delicious food you love so well. Even now I am eating a caramel pastry and sighing for you.

There was a small stain of caramel on the page and Prince Eugene longed to lick it from the paper, but thought it beneath him. Instead, he folded the letter and slipped it inside his breast pocket, close to his heart. It was hardly a love note, but it was the best he could have hoped for. He opened his wooden writing slope, laid out a sheet of paper and began to write in reply.

Caramel pastries will make you fat, my sweet...

But every time the cannons roared, his hand would tremble and the black ink formed spidery splodges on the writing paper.

'War is the making of a man,' said the Archduke merrily, standing at the door of the tent and picking beetroot from his teeth with the tip of a bayonet. 'Prepare for battle, my boy.'

Prince Eugene did not want to prepare for battle, but the Archduke bellowed so loudly at his nephew as he marched from the tent that the Prince was forced to submit. The valet dressed his master for the battlefield. As Prince Eugene's boots were buckled and his epaulettes fastened, he pulled on his jewelled gauntlets.

Cautiously opening the flap of the tent he stepped outside. He peered through his pocket telescope. Rockets burst high above the distant battlefield and he clutched his head as though his brain had been rocked inside his skull. He slipped the telescope into his pocket and retreated rapidly back inside the tent.

'If that is war,' observed the Prince, 'then I want nothing to do with it.'

'Majesty,' said Kayakovsky, placing a small velvet casket on the desk. 'A parting gift from the boy Kalvitas.'

Prince Eugene almost cried as he lifted the lid and

inhaled the fragrant aroma of cocoa. Without removing his boots he climbed back into bed, holding the casket tightly in his hands. Taking a bite from an ingot of white chocolate, flavoured with cinnamon and oil of orange, he rested his head against the pillows. He closed his eyes as he chewed.

He dreamed of the desserts he had eaten and the desserts he dreaded he would never eat: creamy lingonberry mousses, rich chocolate tortes and truffles piled high on silver platters.

He awoke three hours later, certain that rain was pouring in through a hole in the roof of the tent. It was not. The Archduke was standing over him, tipping water from a bucket onto the Prince's head.

'What time is it?' asked the Prince, sitting up in bed. 'I haven't had luncheon.'

'Haven't had luncheon?' repeated the Archduke. 'That is too bad. Of course, I could send word to the Dark Count's men and ask if they would mind returning tomorrow?'

'Do you think that might be possible?' asked Prince Eugene hopefully.

'Of course not!' roared the Archduke, his eyes the colour of lead shot. 'Now get out of that bed before I drag you out!'

He turned smartly on his heel and strode from the tent.

Prince Eugene's stomach bubbled and churned. In desperation he called for his valet to summon the Court Physician. He hoped that if he was ill enough he would not have to join his troops in battle.

'I think, perhaps, I can soothe your troubled stomach, Majesty,' said the Court Physician, and set to work preparing a remedy. He held out a glass of water and tipped in a handful of powder, which foamed unpleasantly. 'The preparation will help to calm your nerves,' he assured the Prince.

Prince Eugene took a sip of the murky liquid. 'It tastes of mud,' he complained.

The Physician nodded. 'It is *made* of mud, Majesty.'

Prince Eugene held his nose and drained the glass.

'Mount your horse and face the enemy!' bawled the Archduke from outside the tent.

Kayakovsky handed the Prince a small, round wooden box. Prince Eugene lifted the lid to discover that the box was full of a fine, red powder. He stared at Kayakovsky with uncomprehending eyes.

'You must rub it into your cheeks, Majesty.' This did not

make matters any clearer. Kayakovsky lowered his voice to a whisper. 'So you don't look like a walking corpse in front of your men,' he explained.

Back at the Summer Palace, Kalvitas idled his time away. With no prince to feed there was little work to be done. He fell upon any scrap of news from the battlefield as a scavenging raven on a morsel of meat. How desperate he was to fight, to face the enemy and cut down Emeté Talbor with his sword – if he had a sword.

Try though he might, even the most willing boy cannot become a hero in an empty kitchen.

PRINCE EUGENE RIDES INTO BATTLE

MAXIMUS PULLED at the reins and snorted. Prince Eugene's face was almost crimson from the powder that Kayakovsky had given him and the Archduke peered hard at his nephew.

'What is that on your cheeks?' he asked.

'Powder,' replied the Prince quietly. 'So my men will not think that I am afraid.'

'Your men will think that you are sick,' said the Archduke. 'Only once before have I seen a man that colour, and he was not long for this world.'

The Court Physician's mud preparation had failed to quell Prince Eugene's stomach, and the thought of being rocked about on a skittish stallion as it galloped its way across the battlefield did little to calm his troubled mind.

'Well?' said the Archduke. 'Let us not keep the Dark Count waiting.'

Prince Eugene tried in vain to stop his legs from

quivering as he sat in the saddle, staring hard at the Dark Count's army which stood motionless on the crest of a distant hill.

The Archduke passed the Prince his silver hip flask. 'Here,' he said. 'Have a drink of this.'

'What's in it?' asked Prince Eugene suspiciously, as he unscrewed the flask and held it to his nose.

'Hot pepper schnapps,' replied the Archduke. 'Drink it.'

'Doesn't it rot the gut?' asked the Prince.

The Archduke emitted a violent burst of laughter. 'I'm sure a bullet will get you before the schnapps ever does!'

The schnapps made the Prince's eyes water and he gasped as he drank.

'Some men are born heroic,' said the Archduke. 'Others have heroism thrust upon them.'

'And which am I?' asked Prince Eugene.

'Neither, probably,' snorted the Archduke.

The Master-at-Arms approached on horseback. 'Your men are demanding a speech, Majesty,' he called.

'Do my men like poetry?' asked the Prince.

'No,' replied the Archduke shortly. 'They do not.' He pulled up the reins of his horse and started away.

Prince Eugene turned to face his troops. They were a motley assortment of men and many were smoking briar pipes or drinking from bottles of rye beer as they waited for battle to commence.

'Men!' began Prince Eugene. But he could not think how best to continue. The troops seemed oafish and unmannerly, so the Prince recited a passage he knew well, in the hope that it might be instructive for his army. 'Do not clutch your pastry by the crust, men!' he began. 'That is very ill-mannered. Secure the pastry with the tip of your fork. Then, with your spoon, cut away a little of the pastry. Not too much! Using the tines...the *prongs*...of your fork, push the piece of pastry onto your spoon. Open your mouth, men, but please never, ever open it too widely. It is unmannerly to chew pastries with your mouth wide open!'

There was a sudden roar of cannon fire and at a single stroke ten of his men lay dead, without ever having had the chance to eat a pastry properly.

——◆——

And so Prince Eugene went into battle. That is to say, he came close to battle. As his horseback riders pounded across the churned and bomb-pitted grass to face the Dark Count's men, Prince Eugene would trot along behind. And as soon as the mist of cannon smoke descended, he would turn Maximus around and trot back to his tent to hide. Though he did not become a hero, he became a better horseman. Fleeing from the enemy gave him much opportunity to become comfortable in the saddle.

It was hard to convince the Archduke of his bravery in battle, especially as he was never to be found near the fighting. The Archduke took to inspecting his nephew's sword at the end of each day, so Prince Eugene worked hard to gain his uncle's approval by smearing the blade with sour cherry jam to pass for blood.

But Prince Eugene was pining for chocolates and desserts. Every day he became weaker and weaker, and soon he had lost all enthusiasm for pretending to ride into battle. He would slump on his horse, with his sword hanging limply at his side.

'Kalvitas!' the Prince would moan. 'Oh, for a chocolate and marzipan eagle!'

And it was not just the Prince who was fading fast. A diet of pickled beetroot was sapping the energy of his troops. Finally, in desperation, the Archduke gave the order:

'Send for the boy Kalvitas!'

At the Summer Palace, Kalvitas and the Pastry Chef prepared to leave for the battlefield. Frederick and Elka were to remain in the kitchens. Frederick was delighted that Kalvitas was going to war but Elka was crimson with fury that she was to be left behind.

The Pastry Chef watched as a large, metal engine was wheeled out from the stables. It was painted a murky green, with a hinged door at one end and a tall, thin chimney at the other.

'What is it?' asked Kalvitas, following the carriage out into the stable yard.

'They call it a goulash cannon,' explained the Pastry Chef.

'It looks like a railway engine,' said Kalvitas.

The Pastry Chef laughed. 'The chimney is for the steam,' he said. 'And we make up the goulash to feed the troops in here,' he continued, opening a door in the belly of the cannon. 'It is a nourishing meal to ready them for battle. We used it before when I went to war with the Prince's father.'

There were no crowds to wave off Kalvitas and the Pastry Chef, no town band – and this was only right as they were not royal. There was only Frederick and the Stationmaster to watch as the goulash cannon was loaded into a railway carriage. Elka was nowhere to be seen.

It took two days to reach the battlefield and Kalvitas would often stand with his face against the window of the carriage, gazing longingly for the first signs of warfare. He was as eager to reach the battlefield as Prince Eugene was to leave it. But when Kalvitas witnessed his first explosion on the horizon it was almost a disappointment to the boy. He wanted the roar to be louder, the sparks to burn brighter.

So, at last they arrived at the battlefields. Clambering down from the railway carriage, the Pastry Chef took charge as a large green canvas kitchen tent was erected. Soldiers hammered iron tent pegs into the boggy earth while the goulash cannon was unloaded from the railway wagon and onto the wooden planks to prevent it from sinking into the mud.

'Old friend!' cried Prince Eugene, appearing from his tent, a muffler round his neck to keep out the cold. He held out his arms to Kalvitas and embraced the boy tightly. 'You have brought me my pastry eagles?' he whispered.

Kalvitas smiled and nodded his head.

'Careful,' came a loud voice from inside the goulash cannon, as it was wheeled quickly across the uneven ground towards the kitchen tent.

'A stowaway,' cried the Pastry Chef in surprise and soldiers quickly surrounded the goulash cannon and raised their rifles.

Tentatively, Kalvitas opened the coal door. Inside sat Elka, with her arms clasped tightly around her knees.

'What are you doing here, girl?' demanded the Pastry Chef.

'I couldn't let you come to battle on your own,' said Elka, climbing out onto the grass and stretching her arms and legs. 'Imagine the look on Frederick's face when he realises that I've gone!'

'You've been in there for two days?' asked Prince Eugene.

'I brought food,' said Elka. 'And a bucket for my business.'

Prince Eugene grimaced.

The Pastry Chef frowned, but Elka was there and nothing could be done about it. He lit the fire in the base of the goulash cannon as Kalvitas and Elka set up tables and laid out tin plates. Steam escaped from the chimney of the goulash cannon as the Pastry Chef prepared a nourishing meal for the troops.

Since his earliest days in Schwartzgarten, Kalvitas had dreamed of battle; of the glorious officers with their large moustaches and rows of campaign medals, of the thrill of facing the enemy and returning to camp for luncheon with a blood-spattered tunic and joy in his heart. But the reality of war had so far failed to measure up to his expectations. It was not a string of well-groomed officers that wound its way towards the goulash cannon, but rather a mutinous-looking gang of soldiers, half-drunk, with torn tunics and fear in their eyes. As they approached to collect their food, they sang a song that Kalvitas had not heard before, sung to an old Northern tune.

'Oh, where can old Pfefferberg be?
The bravest of generals is he.

We've all heard it said
That the dear Marshal's dead,
And his horse, Gallant, too
Likely turned into glue!
Oh, where can old Pfefferberg be?'

There were many coarser verses too, but I will not lower myself to the gutter by relating them to you here. All you need know is that the song ended with the following verse:

'They say that a general's no good if he's shot,
But we'd sooner a corpse than the one that we've got,
Oh, where can old Pfefferberg be?'

The Pastry Chef skimmed off the white fat that floated on the surface of the goulash. 'Things are worse than I expected,' he whispered. 'Look at their faces. Like the war's already lost.'

'This isn't a place for a girl,' said Kalvitas as Elka passed by, carrying a bucket of meat for the goulash cannon.

'What isn't?' asked Elka sourly, swinging round and dropping the bucket to the ground.

Kalvitas pointed to the lines of soldiers. 'This,' he said. 'War is a place for men. You should be back at the Summer Palace where you belong.'

'You're only a boy,' shouted Elka. 'What do you know? You're no better suited to battle than me.' And to prove her point the only way she knew how, she struck Kalvitas hard on the nose, sending him reeling to the ground. The soldiers cheered loudly as the boy held his hand to his face. There was a steady stream of warm blood but no snap of bone or crack of gristle.

'That was a hard hit,' said Kalvitas. 'But not hard enough to break my nose.'

'I could have broken it if I wanted to,' replied Elka. 'But I didn't want to.'

'How do you know so much about fighting?' asked Kalvitas, slowly climbing to his feet.

'My father taught me when I was small,' said Elka. She picked up an empty bucket, turned her back on Kalvitas and made her way towards the kitchen tent for more meat.

That night, as the Archduke slept, Kalvitas and Elka sat with Prince Eugene in his tent. They were the only friends he had at the battlefield.

'Imagine this is the Dark Count,' said Kalvitas, holding up a pastry. He had removed the wooden soldiers from the campaign desk, and replaced them with cakes – it seemed the best way to talk of battle with the hungry Prince.

'Then I would do this,' said Prince Eugene, seizing the pastry and biting it in half.

'You have to listen,' said Elka. 'You need to study hard if you want to defeat Talbor.'

The Prince sighed and took a sip of hot chocolate, made by Kalvitas. He idly thought of threatening to have Elka executed for her rudeness, but he liked her spirit. And after all, the pastries were making more sense of war than the wooden soldiers ever had.

＊

Each day, as the fighting came to an end, the bodies were dragged from the battlefield and carried back to camp. The field doctors were long dead, so it fell to the Pastry Chef to perform this grisly task. Kalvitas helped him, riding uncertainly on a white pony from the stable tent. Things were getting worse by the day. The train lines had been destroyed by cannon fire and no more provisions wagons could get through.

One evening, as Kalvitas and the pony crested the brow of a hill and returned to camp, the soldiers laughed as they rode by.

'Here he comes, the little general!' cried a young soldier. 'Sitting atop his battle steed!'

'It's an old nag,' laughed another soldier. 'Better fit for the glue factory than the battlefield.'

'Don't listen to them,' whispered Kalvitas, leaning down to tickle the pony behind the ear. 'It might be their bodies we're carrying home tomorrow.'

There were more bodies than coffins to bury them in, and the problem had become serious.

'And that is why, Majesty,' said the Inventor, Ottoburg, as he led Prince Eugene from the comfort of his tent to the muddy field outside, 'I have invented this.'

A coffin was wheeled into sight by two drunken soldiers.

'It is a coffin,' said the Prince.

'Yes,' said Ottoburg, as the coffin was positioned over a pit in the ground. 'But a unique and ingenious coffin.' He clapped his hands and the soldiers lifted a dummy corpse into the coffin and closed the lid.

'Well?' said Prince Eugene.

'Now,' said the Inventor, 'we do *this*.' He pulled a lever. The bottom of the coffin swung open and the dummy corpse slipped out into the pit below.

Prince Eugene stared silently into the hole. Ottoburg smiled nervously, hoping for applause.

'And why is this such a marvellous invention?' enquired the Prince.

'An excellent question, Majesty,' replied Ottoburg. 'It means that we can bury our battle dead twice as efficiently as before. One coffin for a thousand men! Think of all the wood we will save!'

'But perhaps we will defeat Talbor quickly now,' said the Prince. 'Maybe there won't *be* any more battle dead?'

'Of course,' stammered Ottoburg. 'Of course we *hope* that the war will be quickly won. But...but...'

'You shall return to the Summer Palace at once,' said Prince Eugene.

'But there are no more trains, Majesty,' whispered Ottoburg.

'Then on horseback,' said Prince Eugene. 'We require

no more inventions.' He turned to his valet. 'I will retire to my tent now.'

——•——

Prince Eugene had lost his appetite, though Kalvitas tried each day to tempt him to eat. The war had sickened him to the stomach and he was certain that the defeat of his army was close at hand. He stared hopelessly at the battle map, moving the wooden soldiers backwards and forwards, but his heart was not in it.

'Where is the lazy, fat lump?' demanded the Archduke, appearing at the door of the tent. 'Hiding in here, are you? I thought things would be better with the boy Kalvitas at the battlefield, but I see that they are not.'

'I don't think I want to fight today,' said Prince Eugene feebly. 'I am ill.'

'You were ill yesterday,' snorted the Archduke.

'Well, today I am iller,' said the Prince. 'I caught a chill on the battlefield. I think this morning I will remain in my tent and plan our next attack.'

The Archduke roared and swept the wooden soldiers from the table with the back of his hand. 'You want to play at soldiers when there is a war to be fought?' he screamed.

Prince Eugene held his hands to his face, convinced that the Archduke was about to strike him.

'Look at you, you miserable excuse for a prince,' continued the Archduke. 'To think that you are the son of my own dear brother. I would have drowned you at birth.'

He stormed from the tent and Prince Eugene sighed miserably. 'My men look on him as though he's the Prince and *I'm* the Archduke,' he complained to his valet. 'I should have the man court-martialled and locked up.' But he spoke in a low voice, fearful that his uncle was lurking outside.

Unhappily, the Prince climbed into his bed, wrapping himself in furs to drown out the distant rumble of mortar fire.

It was some hours before he awoke, shaken from sleep by a volley of explosions that seemed to burst immediately above his tent. He burrowed under the covers, breathing hard as he fought to stop his hands from shaking.

There was a polite cough from the door of the tent.

'Who is it?' whimpered Prince Eugene from deep inside the bedclothes.

'It's me, Majesty,' answered a familiar voice. 'Kalvitas.'

Sighing with relief, Prince Eugene emerged from beneath the covers like a rat from its hole. 'I thought it might have been my uncle, the Archduke,' he whispered.

'That's why I'm here,' said Kalvitas slowly. 'I have to talk to you about—'

'He roars so much,' interrupted the Prince with a yawn, climbing out of bed and dragging the covers with him. 'We should put him in a zoo where he belongs.' The canvas tent flapped and billowed in the icy wind, and Prince Eugene sat in his chair, wrapped inside the furs but still shivering from the cold. 'You, stand there,' demanded the Prince. 'Imagine you are my uncle. Then I can practise how to stand up to you. I mean *him*.'

'It's not necessary,' said Kalvitas.

'But I have to be prepared,' wailed the Prince. 'He will shout at me again!'

'I don't think so,' replied Kalvitas.

Prince Eugene freed himself from the furs and stood up. 'You don't know the Archduke as I do,' he protested. 'He comes into the tent and screams at me. He won't be happy till he's seen my head blown off in battle.' He turned to see Elka and the Pastry Chef standing silently at the door of the tent.

'But the Archduke is dead,' said the Pastry Chef quietly.

'What?' said Prince Eugene. '*Really* dead?'

Kalvitas nodded gravely.

'Can I see him?' whispered the Prince.

'There's nothing left of him to see,' said Elka.

And this was quite true. Apart from singed and scorched scraps of uniform and charred bones, there was nothing more to be found of the man.

'We did find this, though.' Kalvitas held out the Archduke's golden signet ring and dropped it into the palm of Prince Eugene's outstretched hand.

The Prince turned the ring slowly between finger and thumb.

'We didn't have to cut his finger off,' said Elka gently.

The Prince let out a low whine, like that of a forest animal in pain.

'I thought you'd be happy he's dead,' said Elka. 'There's no pleasing you, is there?'

'You don't understand,' replied Prince Eugene, holding the ring to the light. 'If my uncle the Archduke can be slain, what hope is there for any of us? We'll all be killed!'

He stepped outside and gazed hopelessly about him. There was a large patch of scorched grass ten paces from the tent. 'That's where my uncle stood?'

Kalvitas nodded.

'Blown to bits?' asked the Prince.

'To bits,' said Elka.

Ravens wheeled high above the distant battlefield and Prince Eugene sighed brokenly.

'Things are bad, Majesty,' called Kayakovsky, approaching quickly from the kitchen tent, his eyes wide and haunted. 'The soldiers are deserting, the horses are fleeing. Even your valet has gone, and the Court Physician. The men that we have left are half-dead and hungry. When the Dark Count mounts his next attack it will be the end of us.'

'But we have no one to *lead* the men we have left!' cried Prince Eugene. 'We are pigs for the picking!'

'*You* must lead your men into battle, Majesty,' said the Pastry Chef. 'As your brave father did before you.'

'Must I?' said the Prince miserably.

'I am certain the Archduke has taught you well,' said Kayakovsky. It was a lie, of course; he thought nothing of the kind.

Prince Eugene mopped his brow with his pocket handkerchief. 'I am not a soldier!' he cried. 'How can I lead an army?'

'There is no one else, Majesty,' said Kayakovsky insistently.

Prince Eugene swung round and grasped Kalvitas by the arm. 'You must become my general,' he said. 'You must lead my army to victory.'

'But I'm only thirteen,' said Kalvitas.

'I can be your general,' said Elka.

'No, no,' sighed Prince Eugene. 'What does a girl know of battle?'

'I'll show you what a girl knows of battle,' said Elka, rolling up her sleeves and holding up her fists.

'A prince does not fight a girl,' said the Prince with a weary smile.

'I'll hit you so hard you'll forget you ever were a prince,' said Elka.

Prince Eugene only laughed. Elka turned and swung her fist, striking him square on the nose. The Prince was knocked sideways by the force of the blow and he howled in pain. Biting his lip to stop himself from crying, he straightened his tunic and mopped the blood that streamed from his nostrils. 'Arrest this girl!' he screamed, and in reply Elka punched him hard in the stomach. She seized him by the ear and dragged him into the stable tent.

Kalvitas and the Pastry Chef came running after them.

'Leave him be, girl,' cried the Pastry Chef.

But Elka was not to be stopped.

Kalvitas groaned. It stung him hard to see his friends pitted one against the other.

'I have to show him how to fight,' screamed Elka. 'Here, like this!' She punched her fist so hard into a sack of oats that the cloth split and the contents spilled out onto the straw. 'You see? That's the way you need to hit.'

'I don't think I can,' wailed the Prince.

'Then you're going to have to learn,' said Elka.

THE GOULASH CANNON

SAD TO tell, Kalvitas had still not been into battle. The most he had done was serve up goulash from the goulash cannon, and drag dead bodies from the battlefield. He longed to see the spurt of blood and hear the crack of bone.

Sensing that victory was near, Emeté Talbor had come to the battlefield to join in the excitement. He could be seen on the distant horizon with the Dark Count, observing Prince Eugene's camp through a telescope.

'What can we do?' said Kalvitas. 'Most of the horses have bolted and the soldiers we have left are falling thick and fast. We need a weapon.'

The Pastry Chef laughed darkly. 'Our guns have gone. We've only got the goulash cannon, and that's no good to anyone.'

'We could poison the enemy,' said Elka with a wry smile.

'If we had food to poison,' said Kalvitas. 'It's no wonder our soldiers don't have the wind for fighting with nothing to fill their stomachs. If we don't have guns, then the goulash cannon will have to do. We'll turn it into an engine of war!'

With the Prince's blessing, Kalvitas and the Pastry Chef were promoted from the kitchen tent to the ranks of the Imperial Army. They worked through the night to prepare the goulash cannon for battle, helped by the blacksmiths from the stable tent. The belly of the engine was strengthened with iron plates, the wheels were greased and the funnel adapted so it could fire cannonballs with each release of steam.

Kalvitas and the Pastry Chef were armed with helmets and swords and they wore the uniforms that had been taken from the battle dead. With their legs wrapped in furs to protect them from the heat of the goulash cannon, they climbed aboard. Kalvitas had stoked the cannon so it rattled with steam. Pushing the cannon to the crest of a nearby hill that overlooked the battlefield, and flanked by the few soldiers remaining, they prepared to charge.

As Talbor and the Dark Count set off on horseback from their distant lookout point, the goulash cannon began to roll down the hill to greet the enemy, all the time gathering speed.

Horses' hooves pounded on the grass as Talbor and his men advanced.

'Fire!' cried Kalvitas. He pulled a lever and as the funnel whistled and belched out steam, a cannonball was flung high from the goulash cannon.

'Hit!' screamed the Pastry Chef as a soldier was struck on the head and knocked from his horse.

Kalvitas cheered, swiping this way and that with his sword. He chopped off many heads, of that you can be sure, reader.

But it was not long before the cannon ran out of steam and Kalvitas and the Pastry Chef were forced to abandon their weapon.

Running back across the battlefield, the Pastry Chef fought to keep up with Kalvitas – but he was too slow.

A voice cried out, 'Remember me?' and the Pastry Chef turned to see Emeté Talbor approaching on horseback, his sword outstretched. 'You saved the raven killer from the guillotine. Well then, you owe me a head!'

— ◆ —

Emeté Talbor and the Dark Count had laid waste to Prince

Eugene's troops, and those who survived had now all fled. Prince Eugene held his hands to his ears and crouched trembling behind the kitchen tent. And still the rockets and mortars rained down.

'The Pastry Chef is dead!' shouted Kalvitas as he returned to camp. 'Talbor has slain him!'

'It's a massacre, Majesty,' cried Kayakovsky, his face ashen and his eyes wide with fear. 'We have no army left.'

Maximus whinnied and stamped as a mortar landed close by. The stallion reared up and galloped away towards the trees behind them.

'Maximus!' wailed the Prince.

'Come now, sir,' urged Kalvitas, seizing hold of a heavy, smoked cheese from the kitchen tent. 'We must abandon this place before we are captured by Talbor's army.'

Kayakovsky ran for shelter, taking with him a large leather bag. Elka followed behind as the mortars shrieked overhead. Prince Eugene did not move. His legs were rooted to the spot with fear. He clutched his toilette box close to him, as though it offered protection from the whistling bombs.

'Majesty?' whispered Kalvitas. But there came no reply.

So the boy dragged the Prince with him. 'We'll run to the trees,' he shouted, tugging at the reins of his pony as they stumbled into the forest, thick with thorns and dry bracken. 'At least we'll be under cover here.'

Prince Eugene fought to catch his breath as they plunged on through the undergrowth, running hard to catch up with Elka and Kayakovsky. Deeper and deeper they ran into the forest of birch and alder.

'Where are we going?' panted Prince Eugene.

'I don't know,' answered Kalvitas.

Prince Eugene gave a mirthless laugh. 'You're probably leading us further into danger.'

Elka swung round angrily. 'If you've got a better idea...?' she hissed.

'Are there still wolves in this part of the land?' asked Kayakovsky suddenly.

'And bears too,' said Elka, shooting a sly sideways glance at Prince Eugene. 'Probably hundreds of them.'

'My beautiful bride,' wailed the Prince. 'What will become of her when I am eaten?' Princess Euphenia was not beautiful, it will be remembered. But war can do strange things to a man's brains.

'We'll rest here for the night,' said Kalvitas, stopping at a spot well-hidden by trees and beside a muddy river. It was a bruised plum-purple sky and growing ever darker. The cannon fire from the battlefield was no more than a distant murmur and he was certain that they had not been followed. 'We're far enough from the battlefield now. And the Prince may be right. Maybe it is too dangerous to carry on through the forest.'

Making what use they could of their packs and coats and rolled-up blankets, they set up camp. Kalvitas tethered the pony to a tree. His heart ached and his eyes streamed at the thought of his dead friend the Pastry Chef – a man who had taken him in and treated him like a son. He wiped his face on the sleeve of his tunic and vowed under his breath to seek vengeance. He reached into his pocket and pulled out a handful of oats which he fed to the hungry pony.

There was no still no sign of Maximus, though Elka searched through the nearby trees in case broken twigs or tracks in the bracken might show that the horse had passed that way.

Prince Eugene took out his pocket almanac. Though his army was lost and his arms shook from fear and exhaustion, he leant against the lower branches of an alder tree to compose a new verse.

Darkness fell as a black cape across the forest...

Rain began to fall and the ink leached out onto the paper. He sighed and closed the book. His shirt was stiff with sweat and his knee was badly cut from running through the thorns. His muscles ached as if he had been flayed and he sank down heavily on a log, gloomily picking the mud from his sleeves.

'I'm cut and I'm bruised,' said Prince Eugene. 'I've never been dirtier. Who will wash me? I have no valet now...'

'Wash yourself,' said Elka, gathering twigs for a fire. 'Your arms still work, don't they?'

Kayakovsky, ever the faithful courtier, reached out for a tree trunk to lever himself up from the ground.

'Sit,' said Kalvitas quietly. 'I'll tend to the Prince.'

Kayakovsky smiled gratefully and lowered himself back down onto his blanket, utterly exhausted.

The thick, brown river water eddied, dragging with it great clods of earth as it swept on its way. Kalvitas scooped up a handful of the cold mud and pressed it against the wound on Prince Eugene's leg.

'You have always been loyal to me, Kalvitas,' observed Prince Eugene. 'And one day you will be rewarded.'

They settled down for sleep early that night, with Elka and Kalvitas taking turns as sentry. Bats chattered overhead and Prince Eugene winced at the noise, though it was better than the burst of cannon fire.

—◆—

The next morning, Kalvitas rose early. An unwholesome fog had descended on the forest and light filtered eerily through the branches of the trees. Elka crouched beside the campfire, blowing gently on the smouldering embers and piling on more wood. Kalvitas suspended his battle helmet above the fire and set to work boiling water.

'Is there nobody to dress me?' asked Prince Eugene. His voice was hollow and it was difficult for his tongue to form the words.

'Dress yourself,' said Elka. 'We're too busy to look after you.'

Kayakovsky climbed to his feet but the Prince waved

him away. 'Is that coffee?' he asked, sniffing hard.

'It is,' answered Elka, emptying the contents of the helmet into tin cups. 'But this is the last we have, so sip it slowly.'

Kalvitas gave a sudden laugh. 'Look!' he cried, pointing at the ground. 'Food!'

'If you think I'm going to eat mud, then you're wrong,' said Prince Eugene.

Kalvitas shook his head and dug his hand into the rough earth, dragging out a beetroot by its stalk.

'I'd rather eat mud,' said Prince Eugene grimly.

Elka scraped up a clod of earth and held it out to the Prince in the palm of her hand. 'Eat all you want,' she said.

Prince Eugene snorted and turned his back.

'But we have cheese,' said Kayakovsky hungrily. 'Why not eat that instead?'

'The cheese will be for supper,' said Elka. 'We have to ration the food we have left.'

She filled the helmet with water from the river. Kalvitas washed and trimmed the beetroot and plunged it into the bubbling water. He stirred a scraping of butter in a frying pan from his pack, chopped the last remaining onion and browned it in the sizzling fat. It would not make much of a breakfast, but a mouthful was as good as a banquet to a hungry man.

Prince Eugene shook a large beetle from his sleeve and stood up to stretch his aching legs. Glowering at Elka, he began to dress himself. His hands were dry and cracked and he gasped in pain as he pulled on his gauntlets. He had lost so much weight since he set out for war that his uniform and overcoat engulfed him. The leather of his boots had worn thin, his hat was battered and shapeless and his battle helmet was cracked. He made his way towards the fire, stopping to observe a spider web that had been cast between two branches.

'This spider shall serve as my example in life,' he said, peering hard at the long-legged creature. 'See how industrious he is, waiting as this moth struggles against the sticky web, biding his time before he strikes. As I shall bide my time before striking back against Emeté Talbor.'

Elka gave a snorting laugh and shook her head.

The Prince watched with fascination as the spider seized its prey. But though it succeeded in binding the death's-head moth in silk, the spider was exhausted by the effort. It drew its legs across its body and died. Prince Eugene sighed.

Elka thrust a tin plate at him.

'It's dirty,' grunted the Prince, throwing the plate to the ground. 'I won't eat my food from that.'

'Then you'll starve,' said Elka, picking up the plate and forcing it back into the Prince's hands.

'You hear the way she talks to me?' said the Prince to Kalvitas. 'She has no respect.'

'You have to earn respect,' replied Elka.

Kalvitas bit his lip and said nothing.

Prince Eugene opened his toilette box, took out the silver salt cellar, and seasoned the scarlet beetroot slices.

They ate in silence and, as they finished, Prince Eugene got up to wash in the muddy river. The silt stung his eyes and his hat was almost swept away by the fast-running water. He waded out further and found that fish were swimming between his legs.

'Fish!' he cried. 'Blue trout!'

'You have done well, Majesty,' said Kayakovsky, who was sitting on a rock, attempting to find their place on a map.

Kalvitas sat beside the fire, whittling away at the end of a long stick until it was needle-sharp. He followed the Prince into the river and together they speared two blue trout.

'I have found us *real* food!' laughed Prince Eugene as they carried the fish back to the encampment. 'We can have another breakfast now. Not just beetroot and onion!'

'Where is Kayakovsky?' asked Kalvitas, looking around for the man.

'He went to relieve himself,' said Elka.

'But there's no lavatory paper,' said the Prince in surprise.

'There's moss,' said Elka, stoking up the campfire.

Kalvitas showed Prince Eugene how to gut and clean the fish as Elka mixed up a stuffing of dried lingonberries from her pack with wild dill foraged from the river bank. Kalvitas skewered the trout on sticks and suspended them over the fire to cook. The spruce branches crackled as the amber sap trickled out into the leaping flames.

Kalvitas glanced at a large stone by the fire, then turned and searched through their packs and bags, becoming more desperate as he looked.

'What is it?' asked Elka. 'What's wrong?'

'The cheese has gone,' said Kalvitas.

Prince Eugene staggered forward. 'Gone?' he

stammered. 'What do you mean it's gone?'

'It was here, on that stone,' said Kalvitas.

'Maybe a rat took it?' said Elka.

Kalvitas shook his head. 'Not a big lump of cheese like that,' he said.

'There must be enemy soldiers camped here,' gasped Prince Eugene. 'Talbor's men!'

Elka shook her head. 'If that was true they would have taken us and not the cheese,' she reasoned.

'If there is no cheese, mushrooms will be good instead,' said Kalvitas, working hard to remain cheerful. 'There must be some, if we search.'

The Prince frowned. 'I'm too tired to hunt,' he said. 'Though I have myself published a small and favourably reviewed book on the flora and fauna of this land, with a whole chapter given over to mushrooms and other fungi.'

'It is an excellent book,' said Kalvitas, who had never read it. 'I only wish we had a copy here to guide us.'

The Prince was stirred with pride. 'You may not have the book,' he observed grandly, 'but you have something better still – the author. Maybe I am not so tired after all.' He took his hat and a knife and set off into the undergrowth, followed closely by Elka and Kalvitas.

'You're certain you know which are poisonous and which are not?' asked Elka, as Prince Eugene cut the fronds of a mushroom from a tree and dropped them into his upturned hat.

'This,' said the Prince, 'is the best and meatiest of all mushrooms. Fried in a pan it will be better than beefsteak.'

Suddenly there was a cry from up ahead.

'I told you!' shrieked Prince Eugene. 'I said there were soldiers here.'

'Shut up!' hissed Elka, and held her hand to the Prince's mouth, her heart pounding hard in her chest.

There came another cry.

'It sounds like Kayakovsky,' whispered Kalvitas.

They stood in silence, waiting for the rustle of leaves or the snap of twigs that might tell of advancing soldiers. But no noise came, except a further loud cry from Kayakovsky.

Cautiously, Kalvitas made his way through the bracken and Elka and Prince Eugene followed quietly behind.

Beside a tree lay Kayakovsky, clutching his hand tight against his stomach, a froth of white bubbles forming at the corners of his mouth. But there were no soldiers to be seen.

'What's wrong with him?' asked Elka.

Kayakovsky's fingers were wrapped around the stalk of a bright yellow mushroom, which Prince Eugene dashed from the man's hand.

'Don't you see?' he cried. 'They're poisonous!'

'What is it?' asked Kalvitas. 'What has he eaten?'

'Death-Comes-Quickly,' answered the Prince. 'The most dangerous of all forest mushrooms.'

'I was hungry,' groaned Kayakovsky. 'I've never seen a mushroom so delicious to the eye and I had...I had to...' Again the wretched man cried out in pain.

Elka looked down. Kayakovsky's leather bag lay open at his side, and the missing cheese had tumbled out into the undergrowth.

'We've found our thief,' she said, picking up the cheese and wiping it clean of rotting leaves and lichen.

'I'm sorry, Majesty...' gasped Kayakovsky. He gave another convulsive moan and clutched at Kalvitas's hand, pulling the boy so close that he could smell the poisonous mushroom on the man's breath. 'If I die, take care of the Prince for me,' he panted.

'Don't speak now,' said Kalvitas quietly. 'Save your strength.'

'You're not going to die,' said Elka. 'You'll be sick, but you won't die.' She turned to Prince Eugene. 'Will he?'

But Prince Eugene's face had lost its usual colour and he seemed grey about the eyes.

'Promise me?' insisted Kayakovsky. 'Promise me you'll look after him?'

Kalvitas nodded slowly. 'I promise I will take care of Prince Eugene.'

Kayakovsky gave a faint smile of relief and closed his eyes, breathing heavily.

'Is he going to die?' whispered Elka.

'He is mortally sick,' said Prince Eugene. 'There can be no more than two days' life in him.'

But death came even more quickly than Prince Eugene imagined. The very next morning, as the cold rays of dawn light felt their way through the canopy of branches, Kayakovsky's body was tortured by spasms and he writhed on the ground. He frothed at the mouth, gave a bullfrog croak and lay still, stretched out on the moss.

'What a sorry end to the man,' whispered Prince

Eugene, lowering his head and resting his hand gently on Kayakovsky's chest. 'My faithful attendant and loyal advisor.'

Kayakovsky was buried by the roots of a great spruce tree, and covered over with soil and moss.

———⚬———

Meanwhile, what had become of the Dowager Princess and Ambassador Volkoff? Rumours had reached Bagelbof that Prince Eugene had been slain in battle, but he was wise not to pass this information to the Prince's scheming mother. However, as no word had arrived from Kayakovsky or the Prince in days, the Dowager was already making plans to take her son's place on the throne, with Volkoff at her side.

Princess Euphenia, who sensed death wherever she turned, was the happiest of them all.

———⚬———

Though their hearts were heavy, Prince Eugene, Kalvitas and Elka continued on their way, eating slices of smoked cheese as they went. Quite where their journey would take them they could not be sure. Seventy-five years ago the forests grew more densely about this region than they do today, and with no path to guide them through the trees they stumbled blindly on. The attentive reader (and I trust you are such a reader – if not you would do well to put this book to one side and turn instead to a tale with fewer and less complicated words on its pages) may of course be thinking, 'What of Kayakovsky's map? Will that not give aid to our weary travellers?' The sorry truth of the matter is as simple as it is unfortunate. The map had been dropped in the undergrowth by the noble Kayakovsky and was impossible to find.

'Where are you taking us?' whined Prince Eugene, as Kalvitas cut at the thorns and bracken with his sword, leading the pony behind him. 'You may be guiding us closer to danger than to safety.'

'If you'd rather we left you here for the wolves to eat—' began Elka.

'I merely wish to know where we are headed,' said Prince Eugene hurriedly. 'I have no wish to remain behind as wolf meat.'

'Tell him then, Kalvitas,' said Elka. 'Tell him where we're going.'

'To Schwartzgarten, Majesty,' said Kalvitas, swinging his sword and hacking at a ferocious twist of thorns. He might as well have answered, 'To the moon, Majesty'; it seemed just as improbable. There was a greater chance that they would live out the rest of their days trapped inside the forest.

'To Schwartzgarten?' gasped Prince Eugene. 'But why there?'

In truth, Kalvitas did not know why he had answered Schwartzgarten. But the seed of a thought had been planted and quickly took root. 'To free the great city and put an end to Emeté Talbor.'

'Death to Talbor!' added Elka and her eyes sparkled at the thought.

Prince Eugene stopped to suck his thumb which he had ensnared on a thorn. 'But there are only three of us,' he protested. 'How can we defeat the tyrant on our own?'

'With bravery and cunning,' answered Kalvitas.

'Oh,' said Prince Eugene.

Elka smiled and squeezed Kalvitas's arm. He smiled back and thought, 'I could kill a thousand Talbors with Elka at my side.'

'If only I knew who Gutterfink was,' said Prince Eugene. 'That would surely help us.'

'He's going strange in the head from lack of food,' whispered Elka.

Prince Eugene took out the folded piece of paper that he had pocketed in the library of the Summer Palace. 'My father left this for me. If I have reason to journey to Schwartzgarten, then apparently this Gutterfink holds the key.'

Elka took the paper from the Prince and read it to herself. 'It says that if Gutterfink has broken his promise then the Prince has to hack the man's head off!' she laughed.

'Yes,' said Prince Eugene. 'That is what my father wrote.'

'Your father didn't know you very well, did he?' said Elka.

'Where does this Gutterfink live?' asked Kalvitas.

'Alas, I do not know,' said the Prince sadly, retrieving the paper and returning it to his pocket. 'If only my uncle, Prince Rufus, had lived to tell me.'

'At least if we do find Gutterfink we might get to cut his head off,' said Elka, hoping that an optimistic thought might cheer the Prince.

Prince Eugene gave a weak smile.

'How is your thumb now?' asked Kalvitas.

'Clotting,' replied the Prince.

'If we are going to free Schwartzgarten, then we cannot rest,' said Kalvitas. 'We must keep moving.'

'Yes, yes,' murmured Prince Eugene. 'You are right, of course, Kalvitas.'

'You will have to be brave,' said Elka, glancing wryly at the Prince. 'Only brave men liberate cities from tyrants.'

'I am always brave,' said Prince Eugene with a scowl, then shivered in horror as a moth fluttered inside the collar of his overcoat.

By nightfall they arrived at the bank of a river. Tied against a wooden mooring post was an abandoned pleasure steamer.

'I can get it to work again,' said Kalvitas, scrambling down the riverbank and jumping aboard the rickety steamboat.

'Maybe it's a trap?' said Prince Eugene. 'Maybe someone is luring us into danger?'

But Kalvitas, who had grown tired of the Prince's endless complaining, ignored him. 'It's a sturdy boat,' he said, disappearing below deck.

Elka snorted. 'What do you know about boats?'

Kalvitas reappeared at the wheelhouse porthole. 'If I can stoke up the stove of the goulash cannon I can get a boat working again,' he said with a grin. 'There's still coal. Whoever left the boat here left it in a hurry.'

'I suppose the crew are dead,' said Prince Eugene, stepping cautiously onto the boat. 'We'll probably find their bodies mouldering away below decks.'

To the Prince's surprise, there was not a corpse to be seen, but instead a well-stocked store of tinned meat and bottled vegetables. While Kalvitas greased the engine of the steamboat and carried coal to build up a fire in the furnace, Elka and Prince Eugene prepared a supper of pickled cauliflower with caperberries and dried salted ham. By nightfall, steam was pouring from the funnel of the boat and their bellies were full.

'I told you!' cried Kalvitas, red from the effort of stoking up the fire. 'I told you I'd get it started!'

Elka smiled. 'So you're a hero after all!' she shouted back.

With difficulty, Kalvitas coaxed the pony onto the deck of the boat. Elka untied the rope from the mooring post and jumped aboard.

Though they hunted hard, there were no maps to be found on the boat. So the next day they followed the course of the river as it wound its way through the frozen land – hoping upon hope that it was leading them closer to Schwarztgarten. But that afternoon, as Kalvitas watched from the wheelhouse, he turned the wheel suddenly and steered the boat towards the riverbank.

'Is it soldiers?' whispered Prince Eugene.

Kalvitas shook his head. 'There,' he said. 'Look.'

Elka glanced out. Ahead, their way had been blocked by rusting artillery guns and the blackened wooden skeleton of a food wagon which had been rolled down the bank into the water.

'We must abandon the boat here,' said Kalvitas. 'We don't have the tools to clear the river and there's no way we can make it past in the boat. We'll have to continue on foot now.'

Elka poured water on the fire to extinguish the coals and Prince Eugene carried their bags onto the river bank.

Slowly and steadily, Kalvitas led the pony from the boat.

Prince Eugene was heavy of heart, but the sight of a nest of chicks in the branches of a tree raised his spirits.

'An eagle's nest!' he cried, peering up at the gawping beaks of the featherless chicks. 'The emblem of the Imperial Family! These nestlings will be a symbol of hope for my return to Schwartzgarten.'

As he spoke, a hawk circled high above them and Prince Eugene gazed up into the sky. Suddenly the bird swooped down, snatching up an eagle chick in each claw and taking to the air.

'Why does Nature continue to mock me?' whimpered the Prince as a whistling wind shook the trees. 'What is the point in journeying on to Schwartzgarten when Emeté Talbor will simply lop off my head when we get there?'

'I had a dream,' said Kalvitas quickly. This was untrue, but it seemed a useful moment for hopeful visions.

'What happened in your dream?' asked the Prince. His curiosity had been aroused.

'Wonderful things, Majesty,' began Kalvitas, snatching up his bags from the ground and walking on with the pony in tow.

'Well?' said the Prince, following quickly behind the boy. 'What wonderful things? Tell me.'

'That we will return to Schwartzgarten in triumph,' said Kalvitas. 'That we will overthrow the tyrant. Isn't that right, Elka?'

But Elka was not listening. In the distance there came the howl of a lone wolf.

Kalvitas stopped so suddenly that Prince Eugene almost tripped over him.

'Wolves!' moaned the Prince.

'Look,' said Elka, holding out her arm and pointing ahead as the wind caught up and rain began to fall. 'There's a place we can hide.'

Prince Eugene followed Elka's finger, straining his eyes and blinking hard as he gazed into the distance. Before them stood a small wooden shack with a rough thatched roof.

'I won't stay there,' said the Prince. 'It's the sort of place where cut-throats live!'

But a second wolf howl caused him to quicken his step.

GUTTERFINK

LED BY Kalvitas, they entered the hovel, lowering their heads beneath the dark oak beams. The walls were decorated with antlers and the floor was strewn with hay. The smell was so strong that Prince Eugene was almost knocked back by the force. He sank uncertainly onto a wooden stool.

'It smells like something died,' he whispered.

His voice was answered at once by another from deep in the shadows. 'Not something,' said the voice. '*Someone*. And I'm not dead yet, though I might be from the shock if strangers *keep* arriving.' The someone shook himself and climbed unsteadily to his feet. 'Close the door,' he shrieked as the wind howled into the hovel, catching papers that were strewn across a table in the corner.

The man staggered forwards. Though small in stature he was made half a foot taller by a shock of wiry grey hair. His beard was long, and was ornamented here and there with pieces of cheese and flecks of pipe tobacco. Though he was obviously beyond his seventieth year his blue eyes glowed as bright as a child's.

'First, know your wolf,' he said, as he observed the strangers narrowly.

'What do you mean?' demanded Prince Eugene.

'I mean,' said the man, bending to face the Prince, 'I don't know you better than the creatures that dwell in the forest. You might be here to do me harm.' His breath smelt so strongly of rotting vegetables that Prince Eugene recoiled and almost fell off his stool.

'What manner of man are you?' asked the Prince, holding his hand to his nose.

'I'm a writing manner of man,' came the reply.

'You are a *writer*?' said Prince Eugene in disbelief.

'Want me to write something and prove it?' said the man bad-temperedly.

'I mean,' continued the Prince, 'you make your living writing?'

'Look at me,' shrieked the writer. 'Look at this hovel. You call this a *living*? I'd be better off dead.' To make his point, he stood and held his breath until his face turned the colour of the mouldering beetroots stacked up in the corner of the room.

'There is no need for that,' insisted Prince Eugene. 'Please continue to breathe.'

The old man opened his mouth with a gasp.

'That's better,' said the Prince.

Elka was staring with interest at a long row of carved wooden bowls that stretched from one end of the hovel to the other. 'Do you keep cats?' she asked.

'I *had* cats,' said the writer mournfully.

'They died?' asked the Prince.

'Eaten,' replied the man sourly.

'You miss them, I suppose,' said Elka.

'You're right, I miss them,' muttered the man. 'Haven't had a full stomach since the last of them went.' At this he wiped a tear from his eye. 'I could make a big, fat one last all week. I've known many a hungry man turn up his nose at cat. But not me,' he continued, and smacked his lips.

The Prince stared at the man and blinked hard.

'Why do you do that?' demanded the writer. 'That thing with your eyes.' He demonstrated to make his point. 'Going blind, are you?'

Before Prince Eugene could reply a wolf howled from the trees beyond the shack and the writer shuddered. He lit the lamps and closed the shutters.

The fire smouldered unhealthily. Kalvitas sat himself down by the hearth and pulled off his boots, wrapping himself in a rat-bitten blanket. Elka too sat down, after brushing rat droppings from a bench.

Prince Eugene stood. He lifted a small book from the table and turned to the inside cover. Written in a shaking hand were the words:

PROPERTY OF GUTTERFINK

The Prince could scarce believe his eyes. 'Do you know who this Gutterfink is – or was?' he asked with a trembling voice.

'Not was,' said the man. 'Is.'

'*You* are Gutterfink?' whispered Prince Eugene.

'Wax in your ears?' said the man, lighting his pipe. 'I've just told you.'

'And do you know who I am?' asked the Prince.

'No. Who are you?' replied Gutterfink. 'I don't much

like guessing games.' He raised spectacles to his eyes and peered curiously at the Prince.

'I am Crown Prince Eugene.'

The old man looked suddenly alarmed.

'"Gutterfink" was my father's last word,' continued the Prince. 'He wanted me to find you, I think. Perhaps you know why?'

Gutterfink shook his head wildly. He tugged a large book from his table and sat heavily beside the fire. 'You asked m⬤bout writing,' he said hurriedly. 'So let's have a tale as we warm ourselves.' He clutched the book tightly as he turned to the first page and began to read. And this was the tale he told, his voice quavering as he spoke.

KNUCKLE-HEAD KLARA

Knuckle-head Klara was a dull and stupid girl. One day, in the corner of the kitchen, she saw a fly catch itself in the web of a spider.

'What a to-do,' said Knuckle-head Klara. 'The spider will surely eat the fly, and so I must save him.'

'Stupid girl,' said her mother, 'the spider must eat, or else he will die of hunger. It is the way

of the world.'

But Knuckle-head Klara did not heed her mother. She took a long, thin stick from the hearth and, with great care, unhooked the fly from the spider's web. And so the tiny spider went hungry. With a brush, Knuckle-head Klara swept the cobweb from the corner of the room. And so the tiny spider was without a home.

The next day there came a tap-tap-tapping at the door of the kitchen.

'Whoever can that be?' asked Knuckle-head Klara.

'It must be our guest,' replied her mother, and opened up the great oak door of the kitchen.

There, upon the step, stood the tiny spider.

'You must come in,' said the woman. 'Through her foolishness, my daughter has left you to go hungry, and so we must feed you with what little we have.'

The best chair was drawn before the fire, and the spider was set upon a cushion so as to reach the table. A bowl of bread and milk was laid before him, and the spider ate his fill. And as he ate, he smiled a smile at Knuckle-head Klara.

The next evening, as supper was prepared, there came a tap-tap-tapping at the kitchen door.

'It is just a branch knocking at the windowpane,' said Knuckle-head Klara.

'What foolishness,' said her mother. 'It is our guest. Open the door, and be quick about it.'

So Knuckle-head Klara opened the door and there as before stood the spider.

'My, how you've grown,' remarked the girl, for indeed the spider's legs were a little longer and his body a little fatter.

'Come,' said the girl's mother, 'and warm yourself at the hearth. Through her foolishness, my daughter has left you to go hungry, and so we must feed you with what little we have. Here is a porringer of soup for you, and a flagon of ale.'

The woman set the chair before the fire, and the spider ate his fill. And as he ate, he smiled a smile at Knuckle-head Klara.

The fourth day came, and once again there was a tap-tap-tapping at the kitchen door.

'It is just a loose tile blowing on the roof,' said

Knuckle-head Klara.

'What foolishness,' said her mother. 'It is our guest. Open the door and be quick about it.'

So Knuckle-head Klara opened the door, and there again stood the spider.

'How changed you are,' said the girl, for indeed the spider had grown so large he could hardly lower his enormous head beneath the lintel as he scuttled into the kitchen.

'Come,' said the girl's mother, 'and sit yourself at the head of our table. Through her foolishness, my daughter has left you to go hungry, and so I must feed you with what little I have.'

The spider sat himself down, and laid upon the table a cape of the finest spun silk.

'Look, Mother!' cried Knuckle-head Klara. 'He has brought a gift for me.'

And with that the spider unfolded the cape, and gently wrapped it round the girl's shoulders, drawing her close to him, so close she could not breathe.

'Mother, help me,' screamed Knuckle-head Klara, 'or he will surely devour me whole.'

'Stupid girl,' said her mother. 'The spider must eat, or else he will die of hunger. It is the way of the world.'

The writer emptied the spent tobacco from his pipe, his hands trembling.

'So the spider ate the girl?' murmured Elka, hardly daring to raise her voice above a whisper.

Gutterfink nodded. 'Yes, he ate her,' he replied, 'and he left nothing but the bones for the good woman to remember her daughter by.'

Prince Eugene frowned and Gutterfink watched him closely. 'So it is an unhappy ending?'

'It was a happy enough ending for the spider,' said the writer.

'I suppose my own mother would not shed a tear if I was eaten whole by a spider,' said Prince Eugene quietly. He stared hard at the wily Gutterfink. '*Now* will you tell me about my father?'

But Gutterfink shook his head and turned to the next page in the book. 'Another tale,' he muttered quickly. 'Tonight is a night for stories.'

As Prince Eugene opened his mouth to speak again, Gutterfink began his second tale.

THE SNOW-WALKER

It was said, in the village of Drammensberg, that whomsoever had died in the village during the previous year returned in the winter months to claim a new victim. This was not a malicious act on the part of the unhappily departed, merely a way of ensuring release from Purgatory. Maybe this was true and maybe this was not, but in Drammensberg the superstition held fast. More than this, the legend had been embellished, generation upon generation adding twists and flourishes to the story until it had grown from a simple fireside tale to become nothing less than a curse on the village.

Jakob was a sickly-looking man, with pale skin and blue, watery eyes. So it surprised nobody when he died—

'Enough!' cried Prince Eugene impatiently, snatching the book from Gutterfink's hands. 'I've had my fill of your tales.'

Gutterfink screamed as the Prince flung the book to the

floor. There was a loud crack of pistol fire and a bullet ripped through the spine of the book, ricocheting off a cat's bowl and embedding itself in the plaster wall.

Kalvitas jumped to his feet and Elka pounced at the fallen book. She opened the cover to reveal a gun hidden in a hollow inside.

'Don't kill me!' shrieked Gutterfink.

'But you are the one with a hidden pistol,' said Prince Eugene, utterly bewildered.

'You're here for the key or to hack my head off,' said Gutterfink. 'Which is it?'

'What do you know about my father?' persisted the Prince.

'I won't tell,' snapped Gutterfink.

'Why would my father want me to hack your head off?' asked the Prince.

'Because I know the truth, don't I?' said Gutterfink.

Prince Eugene seized the man by the coat and shook him. 'What truth?' he demanded.

'That Crown Prince Alberto was a *coward*,' cried Gutterfink.

There was silence in the hovel.

'A *coward*?' whispered Prince Eugene.

'I'm a writer of tales,' said Gutterfink. 'Fairy tales. I don't use my own name...Gutterfink's not a good name for fairy tales. Woolf is the name I write by.'

'I read your stories when I lived in Schwartzgarten,' said Kalvitas with a smile. '*Woolf's Tales*.'

Gutterfink nodded. He reached up to a small cupboard door set high in the wall. Prince Eugene watched him curiously as he pulled down a picture of Prince Alberto, in a silver frame made by Kaspar the Imperial Jeweller, and wiped his hand across the glass. 'He came to visit me, your father. Heard that I could set out a tale properly. Wanted me to write what a brave soldier he'd been. How he'd fought against the tyrant Talbor. Make it all up for him. Fighting men don't have the imagination to make things up for themselves. I've lost count of the books I wrote for him.'

'If it wasn't my father in battle, then who was it?' asked Prince Eugene. His legs were trembling and he clutched onto the table for support.

'Your uncle, Prince Rufus,' said Gutterfink. 'As alike as two pickles in a jar they were, him and your father.' He closed his eyes tight shut. 'Now I've told the secret and broken my promise, I suppose you'll be wanting to hack my head off?'

'Maybe we want the key instead?' said Elka with a smile.

Gutterfink opened one eye. 'Then you've tricked me into telling tales?' he said.

'So my father was not a hero after all,' said Prince Eugene softly, shaking his head in disbelief.

'Do you need to be told everything twice?' spat Gutterfink.

'Will you give us the key or not?' asked Kalvitas quickly, as Prince Eugene grew red about the face.

'Very well,' said Gutterfink. He reached up to a shelf and pulled down a box, which he dusted with his sleeve. He passed the box to Prince Eugene. 'Here.'

The Prince lifted the lid of the box. Inside was an ancient and tightly-folded map.

'A map?' asked Kalvitas as the Prince slowly unfolded the brittle paper.

Prince Eugene cried out in surprise. 'A map of the catacombs! My father spoke of this place.'

'The catacombs?' said Elka. 'What are the catacombs?'

'This,' said Prince Eugene grandly, 'could be our way into Schwartzgarten.'

Rainwater dribbled in through holes in the roof, captured by a scattered assortment of dented pans and rusting helmets. Gutterfink suddenly held a finger to his lips to silence his visitors and pressed his ear hard against the wall.

'They think they can hide from me, but they can't,' he whispered. Suddenly he thrust his hand through the crumbling plaster wall, and retrieved a small grey rat, tugging it out firmly by its tail. 'This one's a tiddler,' he grumbled as he strode across the floor. 'Not an eating rat.' He swung the creature by its tail like a pendulum, opened the door and hurled the rat out into the storm.

'Writing fairy tales seems a strange thing for a man to do,' said Elka, stepping over a large mound of rat droppings. 'There must be easier ways to live than this.'

Gutterfink nodded and gave a cracked laugh. 'If there are, I haven't found them.' He was trying to entice another, fatter rat into the cooking pot.

'What do you enjoy about writing?'

'Getting paid,' answered the man without a moment's hesitation. 'Which doesn't happen often these days.'

A beetle dropped from one of the dark beams of the hovel and landed on Kalvitas's head. Elka lifted the insect gently by a leg and dropped it on the floor where it scuttled off into the shadows.

'We have to go soon,' said Kalvitas. 'It isn't safe to stay in one place for too long. Talbor may be hunting for us.'

'There's nowhere for you to run,' said Gutterfink with a laugh. 'Nowhere for you to go.'

But it was clear to the old man that his guests had made up their minds.

'Better have this, then, if you're going,' said Gutterfink, taking a lump of blue cheese from the larder and wrapping it in paper, which he tied tightly with string.

'Why eat rats if you have cheese?' asked Elka.

'I prefer the flavour,' said the man. 'If I can't have cat, I have rat. And if rats are thin on the ground, I have cheese. Now take it,' he said, opening a shutter and peering outside. 'You need something to keep you alive.' He smiled darkly and tapped at the murky glass of the window. 'Alive, that is, until the wolves get you.'

They waited until twilight had settled before leaving the hovel. Disquieted by the howls of distant wolves, they made their way deep into the forest. The wind had dropped though the rain still fell.

But hunger soon got the better of Prince Eugene.

'I have to eat,' he whined. 'If I don't I'll fall here – dead. Is that what you want?'

Though Elka thought this was the best thing that could possibly happen, she held her tongue.

'And I expect Gutterfink is right about the wolves,' continued the Prince. 'We'd be better off going to our deaths with full stomachs.'

'If we eat the cheese now and we aren't killed by wolves, who knows where our next meal will come from?' said Kalvitas.

But Prince Eugene was deaf to Kalvitas's warning. His brain was whirring like clockwork, and the harder he thought the hungrier he became. His father, Prince Alberto, who had seemed so brave and strong, had been nothing more than a liar, and the knowledge stung him. He swallowed his ration of cheese so quickly he barely had chance to notice the rank taste.

As they walked on they caught the sweet smell of wood smoke, carried from a small tavern set back from a dirt path. There was an amber glow of candlelight at the window and a plume of powder-white smoke funnelled upwards from the chimney.

'Quickly,' whispered Kalvitas. 'We mustn't be seen.'

'But the place smells of stew...' said Prince Eugene, breathing in deeply. 'Stew and pepper dumplings. Can't we stop here for a while and dine? Maybe they will take pity on starving travellers.'

'Stew and pepper dumplings aren't much use to a man if he has no head to eat them with,' said Elka sharply.

Prince Eugene gulped and quickened his pace.

They hurried on through the trees. The sun was no more than a glimmer in the sky and the shadows played tricks.

'There are creatures here, watching us,' gasped Prince Eugene.

'It's only the light,' replied Kalvitas.

'Maybe it's ghosts,' said Elka, smiling unpleasantly at the Prince. 'Maybe they've come to get you.'

Prince Eugene pulled back. Ahead of them a shadow seemed to shift between two trees. 'There!' whispered the Prince, extending a trembling finger and pointing into the darkness.

The shadow moved suddenly and snorted, filling the air with steaming breath.

A voice called out to them. 'Do not be afraid. He will not hurt you.'

Prince Eugene strained his eyes as he struggled to make out the shape of the large, snorting creature. Suddenly he uttered a short bark of a laugh and Elka turned in surprise.

'That's not a ghost!' he exclaimed. 'It's Maximus.'

Maximus snorted again, as if in reply to the Prince.

'You see? He remembers his master.'

The figure beside the horse lit a lantern and held it aloft.

'Who are you?' demanded Kalvitas. 'What is your name? Come forward and show yourself.'

'My name?' replied the figure, approaching through the bracken. 'My name is Marshal Maurice Pfefferberg.'

THE ELUSIVE MARSHAL

PFEFFERBERG

———◆◆◆———

A ND WHAT of the story of Marshal Pfefferberg, you may well ask? Where had he been and why had he not appeared before now? Let the old soldier speak for himself, I say.

'It was on the very day war was declared,' said Marshal Pfefferberg, as they negotiated their way cautiously through the forest, Prince Eugene and the Marshal leading on Maximus, and Kalvitas and Elka following along behind on the pony. 'I was riding my horse, Gallant,' continued the Marshal, 'back to the Summer Palace to receive my orders, when I was set upon by Talbor's men. I sliced at them with my sword and cut off more arms and legs than I can count on the fingers of two hands, but it was not enough.'

'What happened?' asked Elka.

'They dragged me to a cave and kept me prisoner,' said the Marshal.

'And we saved you!' declared the Prince.

'He was already safe when we found him,' said Elka.

'What do you mean?' asked the Prince.

'Well, he wasn't tied up in a cave, was he?' sighed the girl. 'That's what I mean.'

'So how did you escape?' asked Kalvitas.

'It is too painful to relate,' answered the Marshal, leaning down from the saddle to swipe at a clump of nettles with the blade of his sword.

'It was probably very bad,' whispered Elka. 'He doesn't want to tell us of all the chopping he had to do.'

Suddenly the Marshal pointed ahead through the darkness. 'Look!'

To Kalvitas's surprise he saw that where the trees grew less densely, a set of railway lines led through the forest.

———

'If we follow the track,' said Kalvitas the next morning, 'it must lead us towards Schwartzgarten, or to some other place where we might find help.'

'Remember, every tree poses a threat,' cautioned the Marshal. 'Every spruce or silver birch offers the perfect hiding place for one of Emeté Talbor's marksmen.'

The party progressed slowly, following the railway lines all the time, until by the afternoon they reached the outskirts of what had once been a small village, though now wiped from existence by Emeté Talbor's army. All that remained was an ancient stone watchtower that had stood at the entrance to the village, the walls pockmarked and blackened from shrapnel bursts. Beside the tower stood two solitary aspens. Even the bark of the trees had been scorched by cannon fire.

Ahead of them, the railway lines were twisted and a lone carriage lay on its side.

'It's the Imperial dining car,' said Prince Eugene forlornly as they approached the toppled carriage. 'Talbor has destroyed my army and now he has destroyed my dining car!' He jumped down from his horse and picked up a smashed fragment of a plate from beside the railway lines. 'A dessert plate from the Imperial dinner service,' he sighed. 'Just think of it. All the chocolate tortes and iced mousses that this plate once held. Gone, all gone. Everything is wrong now.'

Elka and Kalvitas had dismounted from the pony and climbed inside the shattered hulk of the carriage, searching desperately for food. The doors of the pantry cupboards hung limply open above them – pots and pans and cracked serving dishes littered the ground.

'I've found something!' cried Elka, clearing away a heap of broken plates and triumphantly reaching for a tin.

'Is it food?' asked Kalvitas.

'Pickled beetroot!' laughed Elka. But as she lifted the tin she gave a howl of dismay. It was empty, with nothing inside but a nest of spiders.

Outside, Marshal Pfefferberg was examining the railway's warped and buckled lines. 'There's no way onwards,' he called back to Kalvitas, as the boy emerged with Elka from the dining car. 'The tracks come to an end here.'

'But we need to keep moving,' said Kalvitas. 'We can't stay here. And we have to find food, or we'll starve to death.'

'How will we get to Schwartzgarten now?' said Elka.

'We'll find a way,' said Kalvitas, though his hope was fading fast.

Before them was a patch of cobbled ground that had once been the village square, now pitted by cannon blasts. Rainwater had collected in large shell holes, the colour of milky cocoa. Prince Eugene got down on his knees and peered into a pool.

'What are you doing?' shouted Elka.

'Chocolate,' murmured the Prince, and was about to drink from the water when Kalvitas ran over and swirled the pool with the heel of his boot.

'See?' he said. 'Mud, not chocolate.'

'He's exhausted,' said Marshal Pfefferberg. 'And the mind plays tricks.'

Prince Eugene stared up at Kalvitas. 'Only mud?'

Kalvitas smiled and nodded his head. Unconvinced by his friend, Prince Eugene swirled the water once more, and a lifeless face rose to the surface, winking up at him through unseeing eyes. The Prince and Kalvitas staggered back in horror.

'A body in a shell hole?' said Marshal Pfefferberg with a shake of his head. 'You'll get used to that.'

They walked on from the village and across the ploughed fields of a farm. A damp and foetid aroma hung about the place.

'What is that smell?' asked Prince Eugene, holding his nose in disgust.

'It's pig slurry,' said Elka. 'Pig slurry and horse dung. I'm very sorry, I'm sure, if it offends your royal nose.'

Prince Eugene scowled at the girl and Elka scowled back.

The farm buildings had been flattened but the hen coop was still standing. To their surprise and delight, though the hens were nowhere to be seen, five warm eggs sat unbroken in the straw. Kalvitas took the eggs from the coop, and slipped them into the deep pockets of his overcoat.

It was fast growing dark, so they set up camp a kilometre beyond the ruined village. Marshal Pfefferberg found a stream that still ran clean with crystal water and Elka lit a fire. When the flames died down Kalvitas pricked the eggs with Prince Eugene's golden pimple lance and pushed them deep into the smouldering ashes.

As night fell they sat down to eat and Kalvitas reached into the fire to pull out the roasted eggs.

'Life is like a roasted egg,' observed Prince Eugene, contemplating the smooth white flesh as he peeled off the shell.

'How?' asked Elka.

'I don't know how,' said Prince Eugene vaguely. 'But

it probably is. We would do well to learn from Nature.' He gazed towards the stream, where a heron waded and a duckling bobbed by the water's edge. He watched in rapt silence as the heron gently pressed its bill against the duckling's downy feathers. 'Though Talbor may seem a fearsome tyrant, my attitude towards him shall be as that of the brave duckling to the heron,' continued Prince Eugene grandly.

These words had scarce escaped the Prince's lips when the heron slowly opened its mouth, scooped the duckling from the water and swallowed it whole.

———

By the next morning a hard frost had set in and the golden tassels that hung from Prince Eugene's epaulettes had frozen solid. Clambering to his feet, the Prince brushed flakes of snow from his wispy moustache and wrapped the muffler tighter round his neck. The heron lay dead beside the stream.

'It doesn't bode well,' he mumbled. 'We will freeze to death, like that wretched bird before us.'

'Maybe it means that Talbor will freeze to death

too?' said Elka with a smirk. 'Maybe it's another of your good omens.'

'Good omens do not smile on me, I think,' said Prince Eugene sadly.

Kalvitas and Marshal Pfefferberg were busily padding their clothes with straw to keep out the biting cold.

'I will smell like a horse,' complained the Prince.

'I'd rather smell like a live horse than a dead Prince,' replied Kalvitas.

'Look!' hissed Elka suddenly, pointing into the distance.

A man was approaching over the brow of a hill. Behind him he dragged a small cart on wheels, suspended from which were many strings of sausages. He was a tall man, hunched over at the shoulders and dressed in a ragged overcoat and long leather boots. Around his neck he wore another string of sausages. Ravens circled above him, swooping at intervals to peck violently at the sausages, and the man was struggling to fend off the winged creatures with an old umbrella, which he whirled around his head.

'Are you lost, friend?' called the Prince, as the man drew near.

'Do any of us ever truly know where we're going in

this life?' answered the Sausage Seller, for this was indeed his profession.

'What are you doing here?' demanded Marshal Pfefferberg as the man approached. 'Has Talbor sent you to spy on us?'

'The truth,' began the Sausage Seller, 'the honest, spit-in-your-eye, cross-your-heart truth is this.' He leant forward as if sharing a great secret. 'I lost my bearings. But I'm no friend to Talbor. The man's killed off half my customers.'

'It is Fate, I think,' said Prince Eugene, 'that you have stumbled upon us here.' He examined the man's cart closely. 'Sausages, is it?'

'It is,' replied the man. 'Plain sausage, and pepper sausage, beetroot and garlic sausage...and a nice bit of Taneva Black. All sorts I've got. And cheeses from the Brammerhaus Alps.' He opened the lid of his cart, lifted out a package bound in cloth and unwrapped it to reveal a ripe blue cheese. 'There, breathe that in,' said the man, cutting off a slice and passing it to Prince Eugene, speared on the tip of his knife. 'That's a fine cheese, that is,' he continued as the Prince chewed hungrily.

'Meat is hard to come by in time of war,' said

Marshal Pfefferberg suspiciously.

'So it is,' said the Sausage Seller. 'So it is.'

'Where does your sausage meat come from then?' asked Elka.

'If you don't ask then I won't tell and you'll enjoy your supper the more,' said the Sausage Seller with a sly wink.

'We will take your whole supply,' said the Prince. 'Your cheeses and your sausages.'

'Do you have money?' asked the man. 'Times are hard now. I've wheeled this cart from battlefield to battlefield and there's no one but corpses to greet me. Corpses don't pay a sorry curseling for sausage and my boot leather's wearing thin.'

'Will a golden mitre do?' asked Marshal Pfefferberg, reaching into his boot and pulling out the coin.

'It will do splendidly,' said the Sausage Seller, snatching the money and slipping it into a leather pouch he wore around his neck.

'Then that's agreed,' said Prince Eugene. 'Now stoke up the fire, Kalvitas.'

Kalvitas did as he was told.

The Sausage Seller cut at links of the Taneva Black,

slicing off thick rounds of the spicy sausage which he tossed into the hissing pan, poking at the fire with the tip of his umbrella to stir up the flames. As the slices of sausage browned in the spitting fat, he cut wedges of rye bread (stale but good enough) which he passed to the assembled group.

'Eat it slow now,' said the man, as Prince Eugene sank his teeth gratefully into the thick, dark bread. 'Looks like you haven't eaten a good meal in your life.'

The uniform was indeed hanging from the once-fat Prince.

'Not since we left the Summer Palace,' said Prince Eugene without thinking.

Elka kicked him hard in the shin and he howled out in pain. Before the Prince could speak another word, the girl seized him by the sleeve and dragged him away from the fire, out of earshot of the Sausage Seller.

'Why did you kick me?' demanded Prince Eugene.

'You want to spill your guts to every stranger who wanders across our path?' said Elka, scowling harder than ever.

'But he's not a stranger,' replied the Prince defensively. 'He's a friend. A brother in peril.'

Elka snorted. 'A friend? What do you know about the man, anyway?'

'He sells sausages,' began the Prince. 'What else do we need to know?'

'He might be a spy,' said Elka firmly.

Prince Eugene gave a hollow bark of a laugh, then stepped aside suddenly as Elka formed a tight fist and drew back her arm to punch him hard in the face.

'You can't keep hitting me. I am your Prince,' said Prince Eugene, holding his hands to his face to protect himself from the expected blow.

But instead the girl lowered her hand. 'You're *a* prince,' replied Elka fiercely. 'You're not *my* prince.' She gave Prince Eugene a forceful shove backwards and he lost his footing and tumbled into the undergrowth.

'Why don't you like me?' asked the Prince, picking thistles from his hair.

Elka shrugged her shoulders. 'What is there to like?' she replied.

Though Prince Eugene fought to master his temper, anger crackled through his body like flame. 'I have warned you before,' he said, his eyes narrowing to slits. 'When we get to Schwartzgarten I will have you shot for treason.'

Elka reached out her hand and seized Prince Eugene by the nose, pulling him to his feet. The Prince cried out, his arms flailing wildly.

'Leave him, Elka,' said Kalvitas as he approached through the bracken. 'This isn't a night for fighting. There's sausage going cold and we've got cheese too. It's a night for feasting.'

As Elka released her grip the Prince turned his back and strode off moodily through the trees.

'Where's he going?' asked Kalvitas.

'I don't know,' said Elka.

'Should I follow him?'

Elka shook her head. 'He'll come back when he's hungry. Which should be soon.'

They returned to the fireside, where the Sausage Seller was telling Marshal Pfefferberg tall tales of the men of noble birth who had bought sausages from his cart. Kalvitas watched the man curiously. Was he a spy? Kalvitas thought not. If Talbor knew their whereabouts, why did the tyrant not send a battalion of men to capture them? To despatch a man disguised as a sausage seller seemed more trouble than was necessary.

The calm was broken by a loud howl and Prince Eugene returned, running clumsily through the thick undergrowth, the sleeves of his coat ripped by thorns and his eyes staring wildly.

'There is something in the woods,' he moaned. 'Something chasing me!'

Kalvitas sat up suddenly, reaching for his sword.

'A bear?' whispered the Sausage Seller. 'Or wolves?'

'No, no,' wailed the Prince. 'An enormous beast. A creature of unimaginable proportions.'

They stood silently, staring into the darkness. A quiet panting could be heard, high up in the treetops and approaching steadily. Maximus whinnied in alarm and the pony pawed nervously at the ground.

'Is it a bird?' whispered Elka, clutching tightly to Kalvitas's arm. 'A huge bird, with teeth and claws?'

The undergrowth stirred and the creature appeared, its head emerging slowly through the leaves of the trees overhead. It was a long-necked creature with hooves like a horse and a grey, lolling tongue.

'It's a giraffe!' laughed Kalvitas. The beast approached

and he reached up to pat it on the rump. 'Talbor's released the animals from his menagerie in Schwartzgarten. It must have escaped the city walls.'

'So it won't eat me, then?' asked Prince Eugene.

'How could it get a big lump like you down a neck as thin as that?' said Elka.

'Think of all the sausages I could make from a beast like that,' said the Sausage Seller with a wistful sigh.

They finished their supper by the campfire, with the giraffe as a curious dinner guest. The creature craned its enormous neck to pull leaves and berries from the uppermost branches of the trees. But it was not safe to keep the beast with them. So, after they had eaten, Kalvitas and Elka led the giraffe further into the trees.

'Go,' cried Kalvitas, patting the creature hard. 'Good luck to you.'

With a snort, the giraffe ran off through the undergrowth, lowering its head beneath the branches, and was lost to the shadows.

Elka stooped beside a fallen log.

'What's wrong?' asked Kalvitas. 'What have you found?'

'Ashes,' said Elka. 'People have been here.'

'Emeté Talbor's men?'

'Perhaps,' replied Elka, clenching her fists tightly.

'How long ago?' asked Kalvitas.

Elka raked through the ashes with a stick and a spindle-thin plume of smoke rose from the abandoned fire. 'Two or three hours. Not long.'

'Then we must keep moving,' said Kalvitas. 'Leave no trace that we were ever here.'

Elka scattered damp earth on the dying embers as Kalvitas covered their tracks with bracken.

Returning to their companions and packing up the camp, they continued on their way in darkness.

The air grew warmer, and day by day they were able to remove more and more of the straw that had been stuffed inside their clothes to protect them from the gnawing cold.

What a strange band of travellers they were. First came Prince Eugene, thrashing at the bracken with the dull blade of his sword. Next came the Sausage Seller, struggling to push his cart over rotting leaves and the tangled roots of ancient trees that had erupted through the pitch-black soil.

Behind him came Elka and Kalvitas, riding together on the pony, and behind them, Marshal Pfefferberg, leading Maximus by the reins.

'When we have liberated Schwartzgarten and vanquished Talbor, I will live a simple life,' declared Prince Eugene. The sun was warm on the nape of his neck and he waved a hovering fly from his face. 'No more princely ways for me. I shall become a man of Nature, and will live my days outside, with the sky as my roof and the stars for my candlelight.'

But that was for his future. For the moment, he was more occupied with examining Gutterfink's map.

'Will it show us the way to the city?' asked Elka.

'It won't do that,' said Prince Eugene. 'But once we know in which direction Schwartzgarten lies, it will help us into Talbor's palace. You see, the catacombs are a way of reaching the palace from underground. It was how my family escaped the city when Talbor took power.'

'How will we find the entrance?' asked Marshal Pfefferberg. 'I have heard tell of the catacombs, but I have never witnessed them with my own eyes.'

'Close to the River Schwartz is a small building marked

on the map,' said Prince Eugene, 'and inside the place is a trap door leading down into a passageway that runs beneath the river and then under the walls of the city.'

'And where does the passageway come out?' asked the Marshal.

Prince Eugene shook his head. 'I cannot tell,' he said. 'The ink is smudged on that portion of the map.'

'The map is old,' said Elka. 'The building might have been destroyed many years ago. How will we get into the city then? We'll be captured and arrested and have our heads cut off.'

'You must be brave, Elka,' said Prince Eugene with a smug grin. 'I will protect you from danger.'

Sensing that Elka was about to take a swing at the Prince, Kalvitas interrupted.

'However we get in,' he said, 'we must try to find citizens who are loyal to the Prince. We can form an army to defeat Talbor, his soldiers and the Vigils as well.'

After walking for another half an hour through the dark forest, Prince Eugene found that it was becoming easier to make his way along the path. The trees had begun to thin out and up ahead he noticed a large clearing.

Marshal Pfefferberg stopped and sniffed the air. 'We can be no more than a day from Schwartzgarten,' he said.

'As near as that?' said Prince Eugene, his heart thumping painfully against his ribcage. There was a lump in his throat as hard as a pebble, and every time he swallowed, the lump plunged uncomfortably.

'We must be careful now,' said Elka. 'Emeté Talbor may have soldiers patrolling the forest.'

By the next day they were so close to Schwartzgarten that unmistakable aromas blew in from the city. There was the familiar smell of freshly baked strudel, and the darker, acrid stench of the tannery. Distant voices carried on the breeze and they had reached the banks of the River Schwartz.

Prince Eugene's mouth was dry and his face was clammy. Any fool can be a hero when danger is out of reach, however the Prince was white with fear at the thought of finally entering Schwartzgarten. He scraped hard with a razor at the bristles on his cheeks, preparing to do battle with Emeté Talbor. But his fingers trembled so violently that he could not hold the blade to his cheek without cutting himself.

A newspaper had carried downriver and Elka fished it out

of the water with the tip of a long stick. She carried the paper back to camp.

'It says here that Prince Eugene is dead and gone,' said Elka with a grin.

'Well, I'm not, as you can see,' said Prince Eugene, snatching the newspaper from the girl and attempting to make out the words on the sodden paper:

DEATH COMES TO THE FAT PRINCE

'I am still quite alive,' said the Prince miserably, as if to reassure his companions. 'Though I am little more than skin and bone now.'

A thought had entered Kalvitas's head and a smile spread slowly across his face.

'Are you laughing at me?' asked the Prince.

Kalvitas shook his head. 'If Talbor thinks you're dead,' he replied, 'then we have the element of surprise on our side!'

RETURN TO SCHWARTZGARTEN

O UR TRAVELLERS sat up late into the night, poring over the map of the catacombs and talking bravely of their hoped-for encounter with Emeté Talbor. They did not light a fire, for fear that smoke would give them away. Marshal Pfefferberg spoke gleefully of battle, slicing more of the Sausage Seller's Taneva Black with his sword to indicate the arms and legs he had cut off in his glorious military career. They ate the sausage cold and at last settled down for sleep.

At first light, Prince Eugene was awakened by the cracking of twigs. He sat up to see Marshal Pfefferberg slowly creeping away from the camp.

'Stop!' cried the Prince and the Marshal turned. 'Where are you going, Pfefferberg?'

Elka and Kalvitas climbed up from the ground and the Sausage Seller stirred from his sleep.

'I cannot come with you,' said the old Marshal.

'But why not?' demanded the Prince.

'It was no coincidence that you found me so close to Gutterfink's hovel,' continued the Marshal sadly. He reached inside his jacket and pulled out a sheaf of papers, which he passed to Prince Eugene. On the very first page were the words:

THE BATTLES OF MARSHAL MAURICE PFEFFERBERG: A HISTORY

'I see,' said Prince Eugene. 'You wanted him to write what a brave soldier you were. How you were as brave—'

'As your father,' interrupted the Marshal. He was a broken man and turned away.

'So you were never captured by Talbor's troops?' asked Elka.

The Marshal shook his head. 'History will remember your other generals, Majesty. General Montelmarte. General Bratislav. Old Grand Duke Sergei. But who will wish to remember Cowardly Marshal Pfefferberg?'

Prince Eugene handed the papers back to the Marshal.

'Take this,' he said gently. 'We will not tell your secret. Live well and live happily.'

Marshal Pfefferberg bowed to Prince Eugene and set off on his way. Even Elka, who was often hard on the Prince, was moved by his kindness to the old General.

After a breakfast of cold sausage, Kalvitas led the pony from the camp and turned it loose.

'We cannot take you where we're going either,' said Prince Eugene to Maximus, patting his horse. 'I will find you again, be sure of that!' he called softly as the horse trotted away.

As is often the case with a good plan, it is easier in the plotting than the carrying out. As they approached the fringes of the forest that edged the city, they found that their way was barred by a sentry box with two of Talbor's soldiers stationed inside.

'Here,' said the Sausage Seller, 'hang these sausages round your neck. They'll disguise you.'

'But they won't disguise the Prince,' said Kalvitas. 'He will be recognised at once.'

'Then what can we do?' said Prince Eugene. 'We must get past those soldiers to reach the entrance to the catacombs.'

'You could hide in the sausage cart,' suggested Elka.

Prince Eugene glared at the girl. 'What!'

'It's the only way,' said Elka.

Although Prince Eugene protested, it was the safest plan they could think up to get him past the sentries, so the Prince climbed into the cart and they carried on walking.

It was easy enough to get past the soldiers, by bribing them with their last string of Taneva Black. But it was only when they were safely beyond them that Prince Eugene could climb out of the cart, stinking of sausage.

'And this is where I must leave you too,' said the Sausage Seller. 'I can't be trundling through catacombs with a sausage cart or I'll lose my living.'

'You have been a brave companion,' said the Prince and shook the man's hand warmly.

The Sausage Seller took his leave of them and the travellers continued on their way.

'I told you the Sausage Seller was no spy,' grinned the Prince.

'Are you sure you know where you're going?' asked Elka moodily.

'Gutterfink's map will show us the way,' replied the Prince.

After walking for many minutes the Prince let out a muffled cry of delight.

Ahead of them was a small building that had once been a tea pavilion for the Imperial Family when they picnicked in the forest.

'Come!' said Prince Eugene, leading the way inside. 'This is our way back into the palace.' The walls were panelled in oak, and morning light filtered in through woodworm holes in the shutters. 'It must have been pleasant here once,' said the Prince. 'Time has changed this place.' On a table there were remnants of a meal recently eaten and Prince Eugene watched in disgust as rats dragged the meat bones back to their holes.

'Well?' said Elka. 'Where is the entrance to the catacombs?'

Prince Eugene stared hard at Gutterfink's map and felt around on the dusty floor. He found a concealed ring in a plank of wood and pulled hard, revealing steps into a cellar below. There were still lanterns in a cupboard in the tea pavilion, and with a flint from his pocket Kalvitas was able to light them.

They climbed down into the hole and pulled the

rapdoor shut above their heads. In the floor of the cellar
vas another hidden door, as marked on Gutterfink's
nap, and climbing down an old iron ladder they found
hemselves in a stone passageway.

'The catacombs were constructed in the days of
Emperor Xavier,' explained Prince Eugene as he led Elka
ind Kalvitas onwards. 'Over three hundred years ago. Now
luck your heads, the ceiling grows lower as we pass beneath
he River Schwartz.'

The stone ceiling glistened from the damp and the tunnels
vere deep with foul-smelling water, which seeped in over
he tops of the Prince's leather riding boots and squelched
inpleasantly as he walked.

The passage grew quickly narrower and Kalvitas held
ip his lantern to light the map so that they could choose the
orrect passages through the winding labyrinth.

As they finally reached the end of the tunnels, their way
vas blocked by a locked door. It was stoutly made of oak and
io matter how hard they forced their shoulders against it, the
loor could not be opened.

'What do we do now?' asked Elka.

'This must be a different passage from the one my family

used when they fled Schwartzgarten,' said Prince Eugene. 'If only we had a key.'

'What do you have in your toilette box?' asked Kalvitas suddenly.

'Very little that is of use,' said the Prince.

'Perhaps we can pick the lock,' said Kalvitas. 'My father showed me a hundred times how to do it, before his hands got bad from the schnapps.'

'There's my button hook,' said Prince Eugene, lifting the object from his box. 'Would that help?'

Kalvitas smiled and carefully inserted the hook into the lock. But though he wriggled and twisted the silver hook, the lock was too stiff to move.

'If only we had something to grease it with,' said Kalvitas.

Silently, Prince Eugene handed Kalvitas his golden flask of earwax.

As the door swung open they discovered a stone staircase winding upwards, so narrow that they could only climb one at a time. Kalvitas was troubled – though they had thought long and hard of their return to the city, the closer they came to the palace, the more impossible it seemed that Talbor could ever be defeated. They were little more than children and Talbor was a tyrant.

The stairway led up into a small wooden chamber.

'Where are we now, I wonder?' asked Prince Eugene, peering at the map, but Elka held her hands tight over the Prince's mouth to silence him.

In a moment of anger Prince Eugene considered biting Elka's fingers, but he suddenly noticed that light was shining through a hole in the wall of the room. Peering through the hole, he could make out a figure – a figure with long dark hair and piercing black eyes. The figure was alone, walking slowly around the room and staring up admiringly at many hundreds of grisly paintings that hung from the wall.

'Heads!' gasped Prince Eugene, leaning hard against the wall of the wooden chamber, which swung open, depositing him in a heap on the marble floor of the palace gymnasium beside Talbor's guillotine.

DEATH TO THE TYRANT!

EMETÉ TALBOR swung round and glared at his unexpected visitors. A smile bled slowly across his face.

'Like rats that have scuttled up from the sewers.'

At the mention of rats, Talbor's hounds Hubris and Nemesis, lying sprawled on the floor, growled and snapped their teeth as they slept. Cerberus sprang to his feet, yapping as he ran in circles round the guillotine.

'You will be brave,' urged Elka under her breath. 'I *know* you can be brave.'

'I am always brave,' said Prince Eugene nervously, and took a hesitant step forward. But the portraits of the decapitated heads that leered down from the gymnasium walls struck fear into his very marrow. The more he concentrated on walking bravely, the more his legs began to tremble. His body quivered as though his spine had been torn from his back. He staggered across the marble floor.

'You killed the Pastry Chef,' he mumbled. 'Kayakovsky

died because of you. And you put an end to my uncle, the Archduke... Not that I minded much about that.'

Talbor gave an elaborate bow. 'And now you are here to kill me, I suppose,' he said with a smile.

Prince Eugene's stomach growled and Nemesis raised his head from the floor and uttered a throaty gurgle of reply.

'That's right,' said Prince Eugene. 'To avenge our dead!'

'Then it is only proper that I defend myself,' said Talbor, reaching up to the wall behind him and lifting down a large, double-bladed broadsword that had once belonged to Emperor Xavier.

Prince Eugene's hand shook as he pulled his own sword from its scabbard.

'Well?' said Talbor. 'Are you ready to fight, or not?'

Prince Eugene stepped forward, his sword arm outstretched. 'Your rule has come to an end, Talbor,' he whimpered.

'Is that so?' replied the tyrant and laughed unpleasantly.

Prince Eugene swung feebly with his sword, missing his foe by inches. The blade struck the edge of the guillotine and shattered into pieces.

'You will have to do better than that,' said the tyrant.

'Or I will slice off your nose, and wear it as a keepsake.'
He grinned and lifted the chain from his neck, rattling
the dried noses that hung there. Talbor raised the
broadsword high above his head and advanced towards the
terrified Prince.

Prince Eugene closed his eyes and held up his broken
sword to defend himself as best he could. Death seemed
assured. But just as he waited for the blade to crack his
skull like a spoon on a boiled egg, a loud stamping from the
cobbles outside stopped Talbor in his tracks.

The Prince opened his eyes. A tall creature appeared at
the window and slowly wiped its long, grey tongue across
the uneven panes of glass.

Talbor laughed. 'Giraffe!' he cried, throwing back his
head in delight.

And as he laughed again, Elka ran forward and pushed
him hard in the chest. He swayed, attempting to keep
his balance, but could not. He stumbled back against the
guillotine, falling hard onto the apparatus, his neck beneath
the blade. He struggled to climb to his feet, but as he did so
Kalvitas leapt forward and released the rope.

The guillotine blade sliced cleanly through the air,

severing Talbor's head neatly from his shoulders, so that it landed with a sickening thud on the floor.

Emeté Talbor had breathed his last.

Hubris approached and gave the head an affectionate lick, which sent it skidding off across the polished marble floor, where it settled on the word 'guilty'. Cerberus lapped up the spilt blood as though it were sour cherry jam.

Exhausted and trembling, Prince Eugene sank gratefully into a chair, mopping his head with a tapestry that hung from the wall beside him.

There was a knock at the gymnasium door. 'Excellency?' came a voice from outside.

Elka ran to the window and threw open the shutters. 'Talbor is dead!' she cried to a group of soldiers in the palace courtyard below. 'Schwartzgarten is free!'

'How can we believe that?' cried one of the soldiers. 'If the tyrant's dead at last, then prove it to us!'

Elka stepped back from the window and turned to Prince Eugene. 'The head,' she hissed. 'Get the head.'

Screwing his eyes shut, Prince Eugene reached for Talbor's head. But Hubris growled and tugged at the ear of his dead master. Only by pulling with both hands could the

Prince free the head, and seizing it by a thick lock of dark hair he held the grisly object at the window.

A loud cheer rang out.

———✦———

Emeté Talbor's furniture was thrown from the windows of the palace, where it was dragged to a blazing fire and burned. The guillotine was also dismantled and thrown on the pyre. The dogs were captured and led away to be released into the forest.

'We need to purge the very smell of Emeté Talbor from this place,' ordered Prince Eugene. 'We must have elegant new furniture, burnished with gold. The gymnasium will be turned into a room of mirrors. Walls, ceiling, everything shall be mirrors! We must banish gloom! But first I must bathe. My time as a soldier is at last behind me. Once again, I shall become a prince.'

The copper bathtub that Prince Alberto had once bathed in was filled with kettles of boiling water, carried up by servants from the palace kitchens.

'What it is to feel free of mud again!' declared the Prince.

A clean but ancient uniform, which had been discovered in an attic room of the palace, was laid out in preparation for Prince Eugene. There was also a golden rapier, which had been left behind as the Imperial Family fled Schwartzgarten. A loyal and elderly servant stood in readiness to dress his master.

'No, no,' said the Prince, waving the man away. 'I can dress myself now. I am not a lazy good-for-nothing. I am Good Prince Eugene.'

The Prince was true to his word, and dressed himself in the uniform, though there seemed more buttons than holes to fasten them.

Food was served and Elka and Kalvitas ate hungrily. There were cakes and pastries, of course, but Prince Eugene shook his head.

'I will not become the fat prince I once was,' he said. 'I will live on fruit and mushrooms...and perhaps beetroot.'

However, the Prince was a martyr to his manners, and ate a single pastry as a mark of politeness. And then he ate another. And another. And he did not stop eating until every last morsel of food had been cleaned from his plate.

The paintings of the severed heads were removed from

the walls, the windows were garlanded with flowers and the Imperial Standard flew once more above the great dome of the palace.

In the afternoon Prince Eugene set out on a triumphant procession through Schwartzgarten, carried on a golden throne that Prince Alberto had used on the day of his coronation. The Prince was borne through the streets, accompanied by Kalvitas and Elka, and there were tears in his eyes.

At length, the throne was lowered to the ground and Prince Eugene stepped down onto the cobbles.

'Rejoice! The tyrant has been slain!' he cried. 'I, Good Prince Eugene, have liberated Schwartzgarten with my brave comrades Elka and Kalvitas by my side. Kalvitas, I appoint you my Court Advisor. And Elka can be Advisor to my Advisor.' He was about to speak again when he noticed a furtive figure moving in the crowd – a figure with a raven face. 'Stop!' cried the Prince. 'We will have no more Vigils! You served the tyrant, but you will not serve me!'

There was a loud cheer from the crowd and Prince Eugene smiled and bowed. A young man reached out to pull the raven mask from the Vigil – revealing the snarling face of Glattburg, who shook his fist and scurried away like a cockroach to its hole.

———◆———

That evening, Kalvitas returned to the house of his mother and father. It was exactly as he remembered it, which was unfortunate. He hammered hard at the door, which swung open immediately and his mother peered out beadily from the darkness within.

'What are you trying to do?' she demanded fiercely. 'Bash the door in?'

'Mother, it is I!' declared Kalvitas.

'I can see who it is,' said his mother. 'Still got eyes in my head, haven't I? Is that blood on your tunic?'

'Yes, Mother,' replied Kalvitas.

'Are you mortally wounded?' asked the woman. 'Because if you are, you can go and die somewhere else. I haven't got room for corpses-in-waiting.'

'It is not my blood,' said Kalvitas quietly.

'Well, come in if you're coming in,' said the woman, opening the door wide.

As he followed his mother inside, Kalvitas felt like a

giant returning to a land that had shrunk in his absence. He watched his mother closely in the candlelight. Her face was sunken and her teeth were fewer than before.

'Hungry, are you?' asked the woman. 'Because I haven't got enough bread to feed another mouth.'

'My name is Kalvitas,' replied her son with dignity. 'I eat with princes. I am a hero, Mother.'

'Not in this house you're not,' said the woman with a scowl. 'And why do you talk that way?'

'I fought in battle, Mother,' protested Kalvitas. 'I defeated Emeté Talbor.'

'And I've had your father to cope with,' muttered the woman disagreeably. 'We all have our battles to fight.' She threw a handful of coal onto the fire. 'Don't think I'm wasting good coal on you,' she muttered. 'I'm old now and the cold gets into my bones.'

'Where is Father?' asked Kalvitas.

'Where do you think?' demanded his mother.

'The grave?' said Kalvitas slowly.

'That my life could be so perfect,' said the woman sourly. 'He's at the Old Chop House, soaking up the beer.' She stopped and eyed her son suspiciously. 'Come to stay, have you? That's your game, is it? Well, don't imagine we've saved your room for you,' she snapped. 'There's rent to pay, and bills for this and bills for that.'

'I'm living at the palace, Mother,' said Kalvitas.

His mother gave a snort of derision. 'That's right,' she continued, with a bitter laugh. 'Think you're better than us now, I shouldn't wonder. All because you've fallen in with that idiot prince.'

'That's treason, Mother,' hissed Kalvitas.

'I don't care what it is,' snapped the woman.

It was not the homecoming that Kalvitas had hoped for. He followed his mother as she carried the slop bucket out into the street.

'So he's back,' sneered the Landlord, pulling on an overcoat as he appeared at his front door. 'The conquering hero.'

The woman emptied the slops into the gutter, splattering the Landlord's polished leather boots.

'I should report this to the Vigils,' screamed the man. 'They'd make short work of you, woman!'

'The Vigils won't be around for long,' said Kalvitas. 'Good Prince Eugene will see to that.' He turned to his mother. 'Goodbye,' he said. 'You won't be seeing me again.'

The woman hacked into her handkerchief.

Kalvitas turned his back and hurried away.

'Off again?' screamed his mother. 'Turn your back on me after all I've done for you!'

But Kalvitas did not turn back. No longer was his life to be lived on the Street of the Seven Locksmiths – he was destined for greater things.

The cafés and taverns of the great city were full to bursting with drunken citizens celebrating the defeat of Emeté Talbor, and the Old Chop House was no different. The floor was awash with slops of rye beer and Kalvitas fought his way to the bar through the thick smog of tobacco smoke. The customers sang loudly and drunkenly.

'Is my father here?' called Kalvitas, struggling to be heard above the raucous battle songs.

'He's here,' said the Tavern Keeper, with a wry smile. 'He's never anywhere else but here.' He pointed along the bar, where Kalvitas's father sat slumped, nursing a small glass of beetroot schnapps.

'Hello, Father,' said Kalvitas gently.

'My son has come home to me!' cried the man, turning to face him. 'My brave boy, returned from the wars!'

'You've heard that I was a hero, then?' asked Kalvitas.

'Bad news travels fast,' said the man, with a smile. 'But good news travels faster!' He clapped his hand on Kalvitas's shoulder. 'Battle's given you colour in your cheeks. War suits you, my boy! Schnapps for everyone!' he cried. 'To honour the safe return of my son!' He clutched Kalvitas by the arm. 'You've got money, have you? I haven't a curseling to my name.'

Kalvitas took a handful of golden mitres from his pocket and laid them on the counter. 'This was a gift to me from Prince Eugene.'

His father let out a long, low whistle. 'That's more money than I've seen in all my born days.' He ordered another glass of beetroot schnapps and knocked it back in a single gulp, wiping his mouth on the sleeve of his overcoat. 'That's better,' he sighed, and sat back in his chair. 'I fought battles once, you know.'

'You never fought battles,' replied Kalvitas.

'I *wanted* to fight battles,' protested his father.

Kalvitas smiled patiently. 'It's not the same, Father.'

'Did I tell you about the battles my son fought?' cried the Locksmith to his comrades-in-beer. 'Gather round and I'll tell you tales that'll make the blood freeze solid in your veins.'

'How do you know my battle tales?' asked Kalvitas.

'Well, I don't,' whispered his father. 'Swords and cannons and arms and legs getting chopped off, isn't it? Tell me if I'm going wrong and set me back on the right path. There'll be stories enough to keep me in free drinks from this lot till the end of my days.'

But Kalvitas had heard all the tales of battle he ever wanted to hear, so he left his father to his stories and made his way slowly back to the palace.

THE CHOCOLATE HEAD

T HE SUMMER Palace was abandoned as Prince Eugene's courtiers journeyed to Schwartzgarten. They travelled as far as was possible by railway and the remainder of their journey was made by horse and carriage. Maximus, Prince Eugene's trusty steed, was discovered safe and well outside the city walls a week after the Prince arrived in Schwartzgarten. Sad to relate, Kalvitas's pony was never seen again.

Prince Eugene and Kalvitas (now dressed in the robes of a courtier, with a row of glittering medals on his chest) stood side by side, waiting as the carriage bearing Princess Euphenia drew up outside the palace. The Dowager Princess and Ambassador Volkoff were due to arrive the following day.

Princess Euphenia stepped down, wrapped in furs. 'I thought you would have been blown to pieces by a bomb or gored with a sabre,' she said, her voice tinged with disappointment. 'But it seems that was not to be.'

'What is this?' asked the Prince, noticing a piece of

paper in the Princess's gloved hand. 'Show me,' he cooed, gently prising the paper from his wife's pincer-like grip.

He stared at the paper, on which the Princess had sketched the Prince lying dead in an open coffin. The floor of her carriage, he saw, was littered with a hundred illustrations of black funeral gowns.

'Did you want me to return from the battlefields?' asked Prince Eugene hoarsely.

'Oh yes,' replied the Princess. 'How could you be buried without a body?' She laughed. 'I was sad to hear that Talbor had his head cut off. He was a funny man. I would have liked to see him once more.'

'You can see him,' said Prince Eugene grimly. 'His head is in a bucket in the palace kitchens.'

Princess Euphenia laughed again and turned her attention to Kalvitas. 'You are a pastry chef, yes?'

'He is my Advisor,' said Prince Eugene. 'My most loyal friend.'

'Yes, yes,' said Princess Euphenia impatiently. 'But he was a pastry chef?'

Kalvitas nodded.

'Then you shall make a mould of Talbor's head and cast

his likeness in chocolate, to prove that my husband, the Prince, is victor over him.'

Though it was certainly a strange request, Prince Eugene bowed in agreement to his peculiar wife.

The head of Emeté Talbor had been stored in the palace ice house, chilled in a lead bucket. Taking a deep breath, Kalvitas lifted the lid. He gasped as he set eyes on the yellow and waxen face that gazed up at him.

Elka shuddered as she pulled Talbor's head from the bucket. With a sharp knife she shaved the hair from the tyrant's head as Kalvitas mixed powdered plaster into a stiff paste.

Holding the severed and shaved head firmly between his knees, Kalvitas began to apply the first layer of plaster. When the cast had been completed, Kalvitas greased it carefully, before pouring in a steady stream of molten milk chocolate to line the mould. As soon as the chocolate was firm and glossy, the head was filled with a paste of pistachio marzipan. The figure's eyes had been cast from the finest white chocolate. Elka dipped a small paintbrush into a bottle of red beetle dye and began to paint veins on each of the eyeballs.

At last Kalvitas reached inside the head and fixed the eyeballs in position, securing them firmly with more of the marzipan. Talbor's hair had been made from long strands of dark spun caramel and the eyelashes were fashioned from the darkest plain chocolate, each lash glued into place with a dab of sugar syrup. Emeté Talbor's broadsword had been cast from dark chocolate, brushed with gold and silver leaf so it would glitter in the light. It was a masterpiece of the chocolate-maker's art.

'That is indeed the face of the tyrant,' said Kalvitas solemnly, as he placed the head on a cushion of purple velvet.

When Kalvitas and Elka laid the grisly dessert before Prince Eugene and Princess Euphenia at dinner that night, the Princess stared approvingly at the lifeless chocolate face of Emeté Talbor.

'He doesn't look so brave now that he's just a head, does he?' she said with a sickening giggle.

The likeness was so distracting to Prince Eugene that he rose from his chair and began to pace around the dining table. But Emeté Talbor's white chocolate eyes appeared to be following him, and finally he cried out in despair, 'Get rid of it! Eat it. Melt it. Feed it to the dogs. I don't care what you do with it, but get rid of it.'

A wooden box was brought from the kitchens, and the chocolate head was packed in straw, hidden from the Prince's gaze.

'What should be done with it now?' whispered Elka.

'Perhaps it could be given to the orphans, Majesty?' suggested Kalvitas.

'The orphans,' replied the Prince, and he clapped his hands. 'An excellent idea.'

And so the head was transported by carriage to the orphanage, accompanied by Prince Eugene, Kalvitas and Elka. Averting his eyes, the Prince unsheathed his golden rapier and the orphans cheered as he tapped the blade hard against the chocolate head, which splintered and cracked to reveal the pistachio marzipan filling within.

'Now,' cried Prince Eugene, 'distribute the foul head among the orphans!'

Good Prince Eugene

FIVE YEARS passed and all seemed well in Schwartzgarten. Kalvitas and Elka grew older and Prince Eugene grew fatter. Bagelbof, who had become ever more convinced that Volkoff was not to be trusted, made certain that the man did not stay close to the Prince – and despatched him as Ambassador to the Duchy of Offelmarkstein. With her ally gone, the Dowager Princess resigned herself to an old age without power and to the approach of death.

Kalvitas, who was now eighteen years of age, dreamed of returning to cooking. And so it was that he and Elka asked Prince Eugene's permission to leave the palace.

'I will never find anyone to equal your bravery and wisdom,' said Prince Eugene with a sorry shake of his head. 'You have given much and asked for little. You shall be rewarded. Ask what you want of me, and it shall be granted.'

'I want a piece of land,' said Kalvitas, 'in the heart of the city. A place where I might establish a new chocolate shop.'

'It shall be so,' said Prince Eugene grandly, and clapped his hands. 'If that's all you demand, I will have it done for you. But if you would rather have riches—'

'Just the land, Majesty,' said Kalvitas. 'That is all I want.'

'Then it is yours,' said the Prince. 'We will, of course, grant you an Imperial warrant.' He turned to Elka and smiled. 'And you will not be forgotten, Elka. You, who have taught me so much.' He reached over to a table and picked up a leather-bound book of his forest poems, which he inscribed with a flourish of his pen. 'A memento to remind you of our return to the great city.' He presented the book to Elka, making a polite bow of his head.

'Thank you,' said Elka, trying not to laugh. 'You are very gracious.' She made up her mind to lose the book as soon as the correct moment arose.

———

Kalvitas took over an abandoned building in the northernmost corner of Edvardplatz. The walls were covered with paint the colour of bottled plums and the Imperial seal hung above the door, bearing the legend:

KALVITAS
By appointment to the Imperial Family

'What was the initial on your coffin?' asked Elka, staring up at the sign.

'M. Kalvitas,' said Kalvitas.

'You should use the M,' said Elka. 'It makes you sound more grown up if you have an initial.'

'M. Kalvitas,' said the boy with a smile. 'I think I like that.'

'The Pastry Chef would have been proud,' said Elka. Kalvitas took her hand and she kissed him gently on the cheek.

Kalvitas painted an M on the sign and tied a red ribbon around the brass door handle. Smiling, Elka cut the ribbon with a pair of silver shears and Kalvitas opened the door to their new shop. His life, it seemed, was complete.

Within the month, Kalvitas had taken Elka's hand in marriage.

People travelled from across the great city to sample

Kalvitas's chocolates. As he dreamed up each new flavour, Elka drew elegant designs for the chocolates in a sketchbook. There were truffles, and chocolate creams, and more delicious sweetmeats than I can be bothered to list for you now. There was even a chocolate named in honour of Marshal Pfefferberg that was hard on the outside and soft marshmallow on the inside.

I would like to write that all was well in Schwartzgarten from this point on, but then I would be lying to you. Many people believe in lying to children, but I am not one of them.

It had caused Prince Eugene great distress to see Kalvitas leave the palace. He was jealous of the boy, but could not tell why. Was he jealous of the boy's love for a girl like Elka? A girl who did not prize a collection of miniature coffins above all else? It was quite possible, reader.

'An opera!' said Prince Eugene suddenly one morning, desperate to cheer his spirits. 'We must have a new opera! I shall write the words, of course, and Constantin Esterberg will compose the music. We will have a festival that will begin with this opera. And every year the opera will be performed, so the history of our great battles will be passed down through the centuries.'

After a large luncheon of twelve elaborate courses, Prince Eugene set to work, and by nightfall he had assembled many pages. Constantin read the Prince's opera and nodded approvingly.

'I am, as you know, a great admirer of your verses, Majesty.'

'Very good, very good,' agreed Prince Eugene, pacing up and down the Mirror Room, with its walls and ceilings of glittering glass. 'The city must ring out with music,' he ordered. 'The people will see what a noble prince they have ruling over them. And what a brave hero I was. My opera shall be called *The Clockwork Raven*!'

———

The disbanded Vigils had no desire to celebrate. They loathed Prince Eugene and wished that Talbor had never died. In the five years since the Imperial Family had returned, the Vigils had become the scourge of the city. They could not serve in the Prince's Imperial Army, and were seen by most citizens of Schwartzgarten as little better than vermin. Many had left the city, but a few still remained. And one night the former Vigils met in a back room of the Old Chop House, talking animatedly as veal steaks and bowls of pickled cabbage were carried out on a tray.

'I served in Talbor's army for three years,' said one of the Vigils. 'To see the way Schwartzgarten has gone to the dogs is enough to drive a man to drink.' He took a large gulp of horseradish schnapps and wiped his mouth with the back of his hand.

'I say we should kill the fat prince,' whispered another.

'That's all well and good,' said a voice, and a man rose to pour a glass of beetroot schnapps. It was Volkoff, who had returned under cover of night from Offelmarkstein. 'But how do you intend to do it, when the Imperial Army is loyal to the Prince?'

'Let us be cunning and break his spirit,' said Glattburg, removing his marble eye and swilling it in his tankard of rye beer. 'Let us strike at something he holds dear.'

'Perhaps an opportunity will arise more quickly than you think,' said Volkoff. 'The fat prince is writing an opera.'

They discussed their plans long and hard and drank late into the night. The candles had burnt down into pools of wax and at dawn the Vigils raised their glasses.

'Triumph or death!' they cried.

One glass was raised less enthusiastically than the others. It was the glass held by Alesander Engelfried.

⋯⋯

Kalvitas and Elka were invited to a rehearsal of the first act of the *The Clockwork Raven*, two weeks before opening night. The orchestra struck up with the overture. A chorus of ravens was represented by the strings section, a disquieting sound which gave Kalvitas a queasy feeling in the very pit of his stomach.

A handsome young tenor stepped out onto the stage.

'He is singing the role of the brave Prince Eugene,' explained the Prince, settling back in his seat as the tenor climbed upon a wooden horse, painted to resemble Maximus, to sing the words which the Prince had himself written.

Elka crossed her arms. 'Does the horse sing as well?' she asked.

'Of course it doesn't sing,' said the Prince. 'It's a horse.'

The tenor raised his sword and bellowed his aria until his face turned red.

Onward, Maximus, my trusty steed!
On towards Schwartzgarten
The Great City of my royal forefathers
That jewel above all jewels
Where my sword shall put an end
To the tyrant Talbor!
On, I say!
There is no place in my heart for fear
My manly chest burns for battle
For the chopping of heads
And the spurting of sticky red blood,
Of sticky red blood,
For the spurting of Talbor's sticky, sticky red blood!

'It doesn't sound much like you,' said Elka to the Prince.

'They were the words I was thinking in my head at the time,' he replied stiffly.

'Why have you called your opera *The Clockwork Raven*?' asked Elka. 'Will there be any clockwork ravens?'

'No, there will not,' said the Prince airily. 'It is a metaphor.'

'Oh,' said Elka. 'I'd rather have a clockwork raven than a metaphor.'

The tenor climbed down from the wooden horse and bowed, hoping that he had pleased the Prince.

'Excellent singing,' exclaimed Prince Eugene, applauding politely. 'You sing the words very well. But you need more bearing, more command of the stage. You must not forget that Prince Eugene is the hero of the opera.'

Elka snorted and Kalvitas prodded her in the ribs.

A stagehand turned a handle and the soprano playing Elka was slowly lowered onto the stage.

'Why is she flying?' asked Elka.

'For dramatic effect.' The Prince beamed.

'And why is she so fat? She's the fattest singer of them all.'

'Sopranos have to be fat,' whispered the Prince. 'If they don't feed at the trough there isn't enough weight behind them to sing as they should. It is a rule of good music.'

'But you're fatter than me,' whispered Elka to herself. 'You're getting fatter all the time. Poor Maximus...'

It had become a very long and very tragic opera and Elka slept soundly in her seat, though the soprano had a voice so high it could have shattered glass. There were many deaths, and each was accompanied by a mournful squeal from the strings section of the orchestra.

'Can't Constantin make the opera more cheerful?' whispered Kalvitas.

'There is no time,' said the Prince. 'The maestro's work will be performed in two weeks. Besides,' he continued defensively, 'no audience would believe an opera without a good death. All the best operas must be violent and bloodthirsty.'

This would prove truer than Prince Eugene realised, as the Vigils were fast setting their plan into motion. There would be a good death, of that you can be quite certain.

THE CLOCKWORK RAVEN

CONSTANTIN ESTERBURG had dined early on salted trout and pickled eggs, all the time making scribbled amendments to his opera score. At last he blotted the final note of music and held the paper to the light. His opera was complete – and this was fortunate indeed, as it was the very night that *The Clockwork Raven* was to be performed at the Schwartzgarten Opera House.

The composer wore a black tailcoat with a red sash across his chest, pinned in place with the Order of the Eagle. Constantin's wig had been passed down through five Court Composers and he closed his eyes as the elaborate curls of hair were dusted with powdered white chalk by his housekeeper.

'The very best of luck, maestro,' said the woman, with a curtsy. She handed the composer his violin and conductor's baton.

Constantin smiled. 'What is this luck you speak of?' he asked as the Imperial carriage arrived to escort him to

Schwartzgarten from his house in the forest. 'A genius has no need of luck!' The steps were lowered and Constantin was helped up into his seat. A copper flask filled with hot water was carried out to warm him on his journey to the opera house. The housekeeper wrapped a rug around Constantin's legs and closed the door. The driver cracked his whip and the carriage was away.

Heavy, dark clouds had gathered above the forest, curling like black smoke in the chill wind that blew from the far-off mountains. Constantin hummed the first few bars of the overture and sat back against the cushions. He ate macaroons as he travelled, chewing in time to the rocking motion of the carriage, all the while clutching the score firmly in his hands. But he was soon lulled to sleep as the dying sunlight flickered through the trees.

The carriage raced along the narrow dirt tracks on the way towards Schwartzgarten. The sun was sitting low in the sky and barely a flicker of light could be seen between the close-growing trees. As the carriage mounted a narrow bridge, a figure with a lantern appeared on the stone parapet and cried out:

'HALT!'

The horses reared up and the carriage rocked violently. The door swung open and Constantin was thrown from his seat and straight into the River Schwartz. Paddling to keep his head above water, still clutching his beloved violin to his chest, he was swept clear of the bridge and into the shallow waters. He spluttered and the dark river water emptied from his throat. He looked up and was aware of a dull orange glow hovering above the surface of the water. It was lantern light.

'Help me,' called Constantin weakly, lifting his head.

The approaching figure reached out his hand towards the stricken Constantin.

'Thank you, friend,' murmured the composer gratefully.

But the figure did not stoop to help Constantin from the shallows of the River Schwartz. He pulled back the hood of his cloak to reveal the grinning raven face beneath.

'The Vigils!' gasped Constantin.

<hr/>

Meanwhile, many kilometres away, in the auditorium of the Schwartzgarten Opera House, the audience had grown restless. Prince Eugene paced anxiously in the foyer, awaiting the arrival of the celebrated composer. Elka and Kalvitas stood silently.

'What is to be done?' wailed the Prince. 'My opera cannot begin without Constantin.'

But just as Prince Eugene was abandoning all hope, the Imperial carriage drew up outside the Opera House. A figure emerged, hooded by a dark cape, and hurried up the steps, passing the lined ranks of the Imperial Army. Under his arm he clutched the finished score for the opera.

'Constantin!' cried Prince Eugene. 'At last!' But the figure did not turn.

'Artistic people are always temperamental,' explained Prince Eugene quietly. 'We must take our seats.'

Prince Eugene led Elka to the Imperial box. Kalvitas was about to follow when he felt a hand on his sleeve.

'Kalvitas!' said an urgent voice.

The boy turned. 'Alesander!'

But Alesander shook his head. 'If the Vigils know I have spoken to you they will cut my throat. There is a plot to kill the Prince.'

'When?' asked Kalvitas.

'Tonight. I would have come sooner, but the city is

crawling with soldiers. When the composer arrives, arrest him. It will not be Constantin.'

'But the maestro is already here,' said Kalvitas.

'Then I am too late,' said Alesander. 'I am sorry.'

The Opera House trembled. The overture had begun.

As Alesander slipped away, Kalvitas ran to the Imperial box. Elka was sitting grimly in her seat and Prince Eugene was standing up, conducting in time to the music.

'You must leave here,' whispered Kalvitas urgently.

'We can't leave,' said Prince Eugene irritably. 'This is my opera.'

'There is a plot against you, Majesty.'

'Nonsense,' said the Prince.

But as the raven chorus began to sing, the maestro turned in the orchestra pit to face the Imperial box. From beneath his cape he drew a pistol and, with an ear-splitting crack of powder, fired at Prince Eugene.

Kalvitas flung Elka and the Prince to the floor as the whistling bullet lodged in the wall behind them. Screams rang out in the auditorium, louder than the soprano had ever been.

'Constantin!' cried Prince Eugene, as the figure made

fast his escape, climbing up onto the stage and fleeing through the scattered ranks of the raven chorus. 'The maestro tried to murder me!'

❖

Constantin Esterberg's corpse was discovered three weeks later in the shallow waters of the River Schwartz. He had been swept against a mud bank, his eyes had been pecked out by the river birds and his legs had been eaten to the kneecaps by blue trout. He still clutched his violin in his hands and a soldier gently tugged the instrument from Constantin's deathly grip.

The news was carried back to Schwartzgarten by the Master-at-Arms. 'We have discovered a body, Majesty,' he said, and presented the composer's violin to the Prince.

'Then the maestro was loyal to me after all,' said Prince Eugene, as he ran his hand gently along the scrolled neck of the violin. 'Why do the people of Schwartzgarten not *love* me? I killed the tyrant. I am Good Prince Eugene.'

❖

Two days later, in the far-off forest, Prince Eugene's Master-at-Arms arrived by horseback at Gutterfink's hovel. Ravens had gathered on the roof and were cawing unpleasantly.

The writer emerged bad-temperedly at the door. A cluster of spiderlings, which had nested in the crown of his hat, were spilling out over the brim.

'An omen of death, when the ravens gather like that,' said the writer, removing his hat. 'It's a murder of ravens, they say. Or an unkindness of ravens. That suits them well, I think.'

'Crown Prince Eugene has sent me to fetch you back to Schwartzgarten,' said the Master-at-Arms. 'And if you don't hurry up, it'll be your own death those cursèd birds are omen of.'

The writer brushed the spiderlings from his hat. 'Death comes to all of us in his own good time,' he muttered, returning the hat to his head and pulling it down with such force that his ears stuck out. 'The grave holds no fear for me now. What does the Prince want with me, anyway?'

'You'll find out soon enough,' grunted the Master-at-Arms. 'Now come on, old man.'

'Not all the money in the world would entice me,' said the writer.

But despite his protestations, Gutterfink was brought to the Imperial court, lured by the promise of plump, fresh cats.

'Bow before the Prince,' barked the Master-at-Arms.

'If I bow down I won't be getting up again,' complained the writer. His beard had been shaved and his hair had been combed, but his eyes burned brighter than ever. Tucked against his chest he carried a sheaf of papers tied roughly with string. 'Now tell me, why have you brought me here?'

The Master-at-Arms motioned to a small writing desk and pulled back a chair. Gutterfink sat.

Prince Eugene heaved himself up from his throne. 'You have the tools with which to write?'

'I have,' said the old man, removing a writing box from a deep pocket in his long coat and laying it on the table. He licked the nib of his pen and dipped it in a bottle of black ink. 'What is it you want me to write, then?'

'I want to be immortalised, in the same way that you immortalised my father,' said Prince Eugene. 'Write of my successes in battle. Tell the readers what a brave hero I was.'

'Lie to them, you mean?' said Gutterfink. 'Like your father before you?'

Prince Eugene ignored him, though Gutterfink's barbed remark stung deeply. 'On the first glorious day of battle...' he commenced.

Gutterfink began to write. But as soon as he had committed the words to paper Prince Eugene clicked his tongue and shook his head irritably. 'No, no, put a line through that. Put a line through all of it. I shall begin again.'

Gutterfink muttered miserably to himself and struck a line through the words he had so carefully scratched upon the parchment paper.

Prince Eugene cleared his throat.

'Sick, are you?' asked the writer, looking up.

'No,' growled Prince Eugene and blinked hard. 'I am not. And I'll thank you to keep your thoughts to yourself.'

'Didn't ask to come here, did I?' said Gutterfink, wrinkling up his nose.

'If it wasn't for me you'd still be eating rats in your shack,' said Prince Eugene pointedly.

'And I'd most probably be better off for it,' returned the writer, equally pointedly. 'At least a man never gets fat on rat,' he concluded, with a sly glance at the straining waistband of Prince Eugene's trousers.

'Yes, yes,' snapped the Prince, scowling at the man. 'Spare me your petty worries. You're here to write.'

'No, I won't spare you my worries,' answered Gutterfink, shaking his pen angrily and spattering ink across the floor. 'I've been brought here under false pretences. I was promised cat, but not a single moggy's come my way.'

'Cats?' said Prince Eugene. 'But you can have cakes.'

'I don't want cakes, I want kitties,' insisted Gutterfink. 'Developed quite a taste for them over the years, I have. Tabby cat or tortoiseshell, it makes no odds to me. But I'll tell you this for nothing, I won't write another word till someone brings me a medium-sized stewing cat and a bottle of beetroot schnapps to spice it up a bit. Grant me that and I'll write whatever you want.'

Prince Eugene rang the bell.

THE DOWAGER PRINCESS

THE DOWAGER Princess sat silently in her robing room. Monette fastened the pearl choker around the Dowager's slender throat and hurried out to prepare supper for her mistress. Alone at last, the Dowager leant heavily on a walking stick as she rose and crossed the floor to gaze from the window. The sun was sinking low in the sky, and Edvardplatz was bathed in golden light. A noise distracted her and she turned.

There stood Ambassador Volkoff. He clicked his heels together and bowed from the waist.

'A gift,' said Volkoff, presenting the Dowager Princess with a box of chocolates from Kalvitas's shop, wrapped with a silken bow.

'My son is still living,' said the Dowager Princess, placing the box on the table and lifting the lid. 'How can he still live? I thought he was going to be shot at the opera!'

'The plot failed,' said Volkoff. 'The boy Kalvitas saved him. Sometimes it seems the Prince will live forever.'

'But I don't *want* him to live forever,' said the Dowager, lifting out a marbled truffle and biting through its glossy shell. 'Can it be so difficult to kill him?'

Volkoff smiled and lifted a stoppered bottle from his pocket.

'What is that?' asked the Dowager Princess.

'Poison,' said Volkoff quietly. 'The liquid is entirely clear. It will not even taint the flavour of food.'

'And does it take long to work?' asked the Dowager Princess.

'Not long,' said Volkoff with a smile. 'A matter of moments should be quite enough.'

'But how can we give it to my son without the fat fool noticing?' said the Dowager, taking another bite of the chocolate.

Volkoff smiled again, a broader smile than before. He had waited quite long enough to continue with his plans. 'You misunderstand me,' he replied, lifting the box of chocolates by way of explanation. 'The poison is not for Prince Eugene. The poison is for *you.*'

The Dowager turned to Volkoff in horror. And as she did so she felt her throat tighten, and clawed desperately at the pearl choker around her neck.

⬥

Prince Eugene received news of the Dowager's death with poise and dignity, though it seemed clear she had been murdered.

'We should build a new cemetery in honour of your mother,' said Princess Euphenia, whose mind forever dwelt on dark things. 'With a grand vault for the tyrant Talbor.'

A substantial plot of land, to the north of the Old Town, was set aside for a new cemetery. Skeletons were rudely torn from their former graves in the east of the city, and the mortal remains of the dead were carried in a grim and solemn procession through the streets of the city to the new cemetery. The Dowager's coffin was transported to the graveside by horse-drawn carriage, exactly as Princess Euphenia had sketched in her book.

'Goodbye, Mother,' whispered Prince Eugene, placing a single white lily on the lid of the coffin as it was carried inside the vault of the Imperial Family. He gazed up at the marble face of his late mother, which had been carved into a wall of the vault, beside the glowering stone face of his father.

Somehow the Dowager Princess seemed warmer in marble than she had ever been in flesh.

THE MECHANICAL HORSE

THE SHOP of M Kalvitas thrived – and every day a crate of chocolates was sent to the palace with a hand-written card:

From your loyal friend and humble servant,
Kalvitas

With each passing week Prince Eugene grew fatter. His uniforms had been altered many times but the fabric still strained at the seams. Indeed, he became so fat that one afternoon, as he climbed up onto Maximus, the horse gave an agonised snort.

'Easy, boy,' rasped Prince Eugene, settling into the saddle.

But it seemed that the Prince's enormous weight was too much for the stallion. Maximus gave a startled whinny and sank forward onto his knees, jerking Prince Eugene from the saddle and onto the frozen cobblestones.

'Are you injured, Majesty?' cried Bagelbof, hurrying

towards the stricken prince.

Maximus gave a final convulsive wheeze and expired.

Prince Eugene's arms and legs trembled as he attempted to sit up. 'Give the horse oats and barley,' he cried. 'That will restore Maximus to good health. The horse is underfed.'

But Bagelbof shook his head. 'A dead horse does not eat oats and barley, Majesty. A dead horse does not eat anything.'

Prince Eugene stared blankly at the man.

'Maximus is dead, Majesty,' said Bagelbof.

'Then have the horse stuffed and mounted,' said Prince Eugene, as ten stable boys lifted him up from the ground.

The following week Prince Eugene visited the Schwartzgarten Museum, passing through the Clockwork Gallery, which was alive with the sound of ticking clocks. A large ormolu clock, mounted on the backs of four gilded plaster rhinoceroses, dominated the room. It had been intended as a surprise gift for Grand Duchess Annabetta from her husband, Grand Duke Boris, on the occasion of their thirtieth anniversary in power. But the Duchess had had a different sort of surprise in mind, and had arranged for a dinner of stuffed quails, heavily laced with strychnine, which put an unpleasant end to the Grand Duke and all six of his daughters (the Grand Duchess had always wished for sons).

But it was not the ormolu clock that Prince Eugene had come to see. On a base of polished black marble, stuffed and mounted, stood the figure of Maximus. Prince Eugene stared up at the unfortunate beast, which gazed back through glittering blue eyes of hand-blown glass.

'And when I die, will they have me stuffed with sawdust as well?' he mused.

Though he was not yet twenty-one, it seemed that Prince Eugene was becoming more immense with each passing day. His eyes were red, his face was swollen and dry as parchment and he wheezed as he walked.

There was now not a horse living that could support the Prince's weight, so the Inventor Ottoburg sat at his desk and set to work designing an enormous mechanical horse to replace Maximus. He rolled the plans tightly and took them at once to Prince Eugene.

'The stallion will be made from iron,' he explained.

'But the principle is the same as with a real horse.'

'Very well,' said Prince Eugene. 'Do what you must.'

For the next three weeks draughtsmen worked at their drawing boards, making intricate illustrations of the iron horse. It was another month more before the creature was complete. And what a creature it was.

It was night and Prince Eugene's stout leather boots creaked and his spurs rattled as he walked out to the stables. There was an unearthly rumble and hiss and the stables glowed a fiery orange. Bagelbof frowned and shook his head.

The iron snout of the beast emerged as the mechanical horse took its first, faltering steps forward. The Prince watched in amazement as the horse inched out onto the cobbles, with Ottoburg sitting atop the invention, pulling levers to control the speed and direction of the horse – either forward or back. The horse was held together with iron rivets, and by moving a lever Ottoburg could raise or lower the creature's neck. A groom shovelled coal into the gaping mouth of the great iron beast.

'And what happens to the used coals?' asked Bagelbof.

'Yes, yes,' piped up Prince Eugene. 'An excellent question.'

'Observe, Majesty,' said Ottoburg with a laugh as he pulled another lever. An iron door creaked open at the horse's rump, depositing the spent lumps of coal, which fell spinning to the ground like glowing balls of dung.

'It is a remarkable invention,' said Prince Eugene nervously as Ottoburg climbed down onto the ground. 'Now, is it my turn?'

The Prince was so fat that he had to be hoisted up and lowered onto the mechanical beast.

'And it is safe, I assume?' asked the Prince as he made himself comfortable in the iron saddle.

'Quite safe, Majesty,' answered Ottoburg.

'And how do I look?' asked the Prince.

'Excellent, Majesty,' said Bagelbof, though he had his doubts.

By pulling the carved ebony lever, Prince Eugene moved the horse forward.

'The mechanism runs along the iron lines which have been embedded in the cobblestones,' cried Ottoburg, struggling to be heard above the hiss of steam. 'The lines lead out of the palace and onto the tracks on which horse-drawn trams run through the city.'

'Excellent,' said Prince Eugene. 'Excellent! Then tomorrow I shall ride out into Schwartzgarten on my new iron horse!'

⟐

The next morning, Prince Eugene made his way from the palace on the back of the horse. He wore a new uniform for the occasion, one which he had designed himself, with a green tunic and epaulettes of the brightest gold.

The citizens of Schwartzgarten watched in surprise and alarm as the gates of the palace were opened and the great iron horse rolled out. The spent coals tumbled down onto the street from the horse's rear to be swept up by attendants. All the time Prince Eugene waved at the gathering crowds, so desperate was he for the love of his people. Behind him, on a large chestnut steed, rode the loyal Bagelbof.

You will know the department store of Bildstein and Bildstein; you might have bought a muffler there, or eaten the sweet pastries that will one day rot your teeth. As Prince Eugene rode by on the iron horse, the Vigils were waiting in an upstairs room. It was the perfect vantage point from which to observe the Prince's progress through the city. Glattburg held a bomb in his hand and waited patiently to light the fuse.

Through the crowded streets of the New Town Prince Eugene travelled, waving to his subjects. At the very moment he steamed past the shop, Glattburg hurled his bomb from the window. It span through the air and bounced from the awning below before landing in the street in front of the iron horse.

The explosion shattered the windows of the department store. There were loud screams as the head of the iron horse tipped forward, breathing fire and throwing Prince Eugene onto the cobbles.

'I am dead!' he cried. 'I am dead!'

But he was not. His trousers were torn and the golden epaulettes had been ripped from his shoulders by the force of the blast, but he was still living. The same could not be said, however, of the faithful Bagelbof. Following on horseback behind the iron beast, he too had been thrown from his saddle by the explosion. Falling headlong into the street, he was trampled underfoot by his own steed, which reared up in alarm as the iron horse belched flame from its rump.

Prince Eugene was helped into a carriage of the Imperial Army which had been following at a distance behind the iron horse, and was conveyed back to the palace and his private chambers, where at once he took to his bed.

'Summon Kalvitas,' demanded Ambassador Volkoff, on whom it seemed Fate was at last grinning. With Bagelbof dead he was at last free to return to Schwartzgarten. 'Perhaps the boy can tempt the Prince back into good spirits.'

A carriage was despatched to collect the chocolate-maker from his shop. Kalvitas set to work in the palace kitchens and carried a cup of chocolate and an assortment of truffles and preserved fruits on a silver tray to the Prince's bedchamber. The rich aroma of cocoa awakened Prince Eugene, who sat up in bed.

'Hot chocolate, is it?' he whispered.

Kalvitas gave a low bow. 'Yes, Majesty.'

Prince Eugene lifted the cup and wafted it beneath his nose. 'Fortified with brandy and finely grated nutmeg?'

Kalvitas nodded.

But Prince Eugene frowned and shook his head. 'I am

too sick for chocolate,' he murmured. 'Someone is trying to murder me.'

Kalvitas made no reply. He could not disagree. He reached out his hands to retrieve the cup but Prince Eugene snatched it back.

'I'm not dead yet,' he protested, and took a sip of the chocolate. He ate and drank then sat back contentedly, sighing deeply.

'Not even another chocolate truffle?' asked Kalvitas.

'Not even another truffle,' replied Prince Eugene. 'As I told you before, I am a sick man.' But all the same he glanced longingly at the remaining chocolates. 'Perhaps one more won't harm the patient,' he whispered, his hand hovering over a plump chocolate fig.

An Arrest And a Death

T**HE FOLLOWING** morning Kalvitas was awoken by a loud knock at the door of his shop. Outside stood three soldiers of the Imperial Army.

'Kalvitas?' said one of the soldiers.

Kalvitas nodded.

'You must come with us to the palace,' said the second soldier.

'But why?' asked Elka. 'Is it the Prince? Is he sick?'

'No,' said the third soldier. 'But not for want of trying.'

'What am I accused of?' demanded Kalvitas, as he was brought before the Prince.

'Murder,' said Volkoff. 'The unsolved murder of the Dowager Princess and the attempted murder of Crown Prince Eugene.'

The Prince wriggled in his throne but did not look Kalvitas in the eye. He was sick, and he moaned in pain, holding his hands to his enormous stomach.

'You have been working in league with the Vigils,' said Volkoff, who was anxious to dispose of the loyal chocolate maker.

'That's a lie,' said Kalvitas.

'You are friends with Alesander Engelfried?'

'Yes,' said Kalvitas. 'Bring him here. He'll tell you that I'm innocent. He is loyal to Prince Eugene.'

'The boy is dead,' said Volkoff. 'Shot by the Imperial Army for evading arrest.'

Kalvitas's face fell.

'An attempt to kill the Prince by bomb, and now you turn to the Crown Prince's favourite chocolates.' Volkoff held up a box from Kalvitas's shop. 'A plump chocolate fig. Poisoned!'

'No!' cried Kalvitas.

There was a sudden commotion outside the door and Elka forced her way into the room.

'Let me see the Prince!' she cried.

'What is this?' asked Volkoff, as Elka approached the throne. 'Why did no one stop the girl?'

'I tried!' said a guard of the Imperial Army, holding a hand to his bleeding nose.

'I am sick,' moaned Prince Eugene. 'Volkoff says I have been poisoned.'

Volkoff did indeed believe this to be the case, assuming that there were others who wished the Prince dead. It had been his own plan to poison the Prince, but once again, it seemed to him that Fate was smiling.

'Poisoned plums from Kalvitas's shop,' belched Prince Eugene.

'He's not been poisoned,' shouted Elka. 'He's just eaten too much. He has a crate of chocolates from the shop every day.'

Prince Eugene frowned and burped. The expulsion of wind eased his stomach, and he suddenly began to question Volkoff's claims.

'Maybe the girl is right,' he whispered. 'Why *would* the boy want to kill me? He is Kalvitas, my friend.'

'That is who he claims to be, certainly, Majesty,' said Volkoff. He smiled and clapped his hands. 'Bring in the boy's mother!'

The woman was ushered into the palace, and knelt before Prince Eugene. Kalvitas grew uneasy.

'Don't cower,' said the Prince impatiently. 'I'm sick of

citizens cowering before me. Stand, stand!'

The woman stood.

'Well, is this Kalvitas? Or is this *not* Kalvitas?' demanded Prince Eugene.

'No, Majesty,' said the boy's mother, curtsying low to the Prince.

'Don't listen to her,' said Kalvitas. 'She's not right in her brains.'

'Five years and he's done nothing for me,' said the woman. 'Not even free chocolates from his shop, curse him! Didn't even invite me to his wedding.'

Ambassador Volkoff clicked his tongue impatiently. 'Yes, yes, madam, that is all well and good,' he snapped. 'But if you could confine your comments to the facts of the case. Do you, or do you not, know the identity of the prisoner.'

'I know his features,' continued the woman. 'Though he's got weight on him since I last cast my eye in his direction. A bad lot, I say. Takes after his father, and *his* father before him.'

'But he says his name is Kalvitas,' interrupted Volkoff. 'You are saying this is not the case?'

'No,' agreed the boy's mother. 'His name is not Kalvitas. This is the Locksmith's Boy.'

Volkoff grinned.

'Then who is Kalvitas?' asked the Prince.

'An assumed name,' said Volkoff. 'The boy was taken in by a Pastry Chef at the Summer Palace. He was washed up beside the River Schwartz, clutching hold of a coffin. The son of the Pastry Chef has sworn to this.'

'Frederick!' whispered Elka.

'And on the coffin,' continued Volkoff, 'the name—'

'Kalvitas?' said Prince Eugene.

Volkoff nodded.

'But I'm not a murderer,' cried Kalvitas, as he was dragged out by a guard. 'I've done nothing wrong. I'm innocent!'

'That's what they all say,' replied the guard.

'It's treason,' murmured Prince Eugene. 'I see that now.'

Volkoff glowed triumphantly. 'And the penalty for treason is death.'

———◆———

The following day, Prince Eugene visited Kalvitas in his

cell in the Dark Tower of the palace. The scaffold was already being erected in the courtyard.

'You were always loyal to me in the past, I know that,' he began, glancing out between the bars. The hanging platform had been built, and the executioner and his assistant were hoisting the gibbet into place. 'But put yourself in my position. What can I do? You have lied to me, you have consorted with the Vigils. I can't spare your life. They would think me a weak prince.' He turned back to his friend and gave an awkward smile. 'Think yourself fortunate it's the rope and not the blade.'

'I would have preferred the guillotine,' said Kalvitas quietly.

The Prince's stomach ached, though it was not from poison, but gluttony. No man, he now realised, could consume thirteen boxes of plump chocolate figs in one day without facing the inevitable consequences. It was hard enough to believe that anybody wanted him dead – but his own trusted friend? Still, the fact that *somebody* wanted him dead was beyond doubt.

Prince Eugene hurried quickly from the cell, leaving Kalvitas alone in the stone chamber – alone, that is, except for the serving woman, who smiled at the prisoner and held out a bowl of food.

'If your neck doesn't break when you drop, your mother can hang onto your legs to finish you off.'

Kalvitas stared at the woman. 'Why my mother?' he asked.

The woman gave a broad grin, revealing a mouthful of cracked brown teeth. 'I saw her waiting in the street outside. Said she'd be happy to yank a leg to help you on your way.'

Kalvitas lifted the lid from the bowl to reveal a stew of grey sausages and dumplings as hard as bullets. 'I'm almost glad they're killing me tomorrow,' he said, prodding a sausage gloomily with his fork, 'if it means I don't have to suffer another meal like this.'

'The things you say,' cackled the woman. 'You'll laugh me into my grave, you will. And these sausages from the Imperial Sausage Seller himself, though they're a month or two past their best.'

'I'll be in my grave before you,' answered Kalvitas grimly.

'Now eat up,' said the woman. 'It's bad to walk out to your death on an empty stomach.'

'Why's that?' asked Kalvitas.

'If they see your legs buckle as you mount the steps to the noose, they'll say it was cowardice. But most likely it will be hunger.'

Though the woman tried her best Kalvitas had no appetite. He pushed the bowl away and stood by the window. Outside, the executioner's assistant had reached up to the noose and was swinging backwards and forwards to test the strength of the rope. The trap door creaked open on its hinges and Kalvitas turned away. He settled back on the stone ledge that served as a bed and pulled a rough blanket over his legs.

———◆———

The moon lit the cell bright as candlelight. Kalvitas swung his legs onto the floor and stood up. He pulled on his coat and peered out through the window. The sentries still kept their position at the foot of the gibbet. He could make out the Officer of the Guard smoking his pipe at the opposite end of the courtyard, thin wisps of tobacco smoke escaping into the night air. He rattled the bars, but there was no way to escape the Dark Tower. Many had tried but none had succeeded. He closed the shutters.

'What will happen to my Elka?' asked Kalvitas as the gaoler appeared at the door with more grey sausages for the prisoner's supper. 'Will she be punished because of me?'

'Couldn't tell you,' said the gaoler. 'Maybe she'll meet another chocolate-maker. One that's not a traitor.'

As Volkoff walked to the Old Chop House that night, he felt warm breath on his neck. He turned to see a Vigil standing behind him, with hooded cape and hooked beak.

'Are you a fool?' he hissed. 'What if someone sees?'

'No one sees a dead man,' said the Vigil.

'Engelfried?' gasped Volkoff.

The raven-head nodded. 'Not as dead as they said,' replied Alesander, and he pulled a thin blade from inside his hooded cloak.

Prince Eugene was heavy of heart. He could sense the shadow of Emeté Talbor stalking him along the dark passageways of the palace. It was as if the tyrant's malevolent spirit had entered his soul, like a butcher's blade through offal.

As he entered the Mirror Room that night, Alesander Engelfried and Kalvitas were brought before him.

'They tell me Volkoff is dead,' said the Prince.

'Yes, Majesty,' said Alesander. 'He was Talbor's spy. It was his plan to kill you and seize power for himself. The remaining members of the Vigils will swear to that. Kalvitas is innocent.'

'You are of the House of Engelfried, are you not?' asked the Prince.

'Yes, Majesty,' said Alesander.

'Your late father was always loyal to the Imperial Family,' said the Prince. 'That has not been forgotten.'

Alesander bowed again.

'Very well, Kalvitas,' said Prince Eugene, though he could not look his friend in the eye. 'You are free. Go from this place.'

'Majesty—' began Kalvitas. But Prince Eugene turned his back and walked quickly from the room. It was the last time he would ever see his most faithful friend.

The Prince returned to his private chambers. As

he peered in through his wife's open door, he saw her arranging her miniature coffins in a wooden display case. A small suit of black clothes had been laid out carefully on her bed.

'What is this?' enquired the Prince. 'Are you collecting larger china corpses now?'

'No, no,' cried the Princess with a hyena laugh. 'For our son.'

'But we do not have a son,' grunted the Prince.

'But we will,' said the Princess, holding her hand to a bump in her stomach that the Prince had not yet noticed. 'With the dark hair and pale face, the sad eyes and the red lips like smears of blood.'

The Prince shuddered and hurried away.

A child was born to Princess Euphenia, Prince Wilhelm, a child every bit as terrifying as the Princess had predicted.

And as was the case with his own father, Prince Eugene came to hate his son. The Prince grew ever fatter and ever more vain with each passing day. He spent hours at a time on his own in the Mirror Room, admiring his reflection and murmuring, 'I am a good man. I am a good man.'

But the harder he stared at his reflection the stranger he looked. The face was familiar, but he was a changed man.

'I am Good Prince Eugene,' he whispered, and the words echoed back strangely at him. 'I am Good Prince Eugene!' he cried aloud and was very nearly deafened by the reverberating echo. In anger, he struck out against the glass, smashing at his reflection with the hilt of his golden rapier.

Prince Eugene watched in silent fascination as cracks reached across the length of the room, stretching out to the highest corners of the walls and spreading across the mirrored ceiling.

He stared above him as a single shard of silvered mirror glass broke away, dropping to the floor with a musical tinkle in the note of D.

As the note sounded, the mirrored ceiling shattered and dropped to the ground – and fat Prince Eugene burst like a balloon beneath the falling shards of mirror glass.

A Final Word From The Author

S O NOW is my tale told? There is little left to say.
To be puréed and pulped and sliced to ribbons is an
untidy end to a life, but that was the way Prince Eugene
met his end. And can you say that he did not deserve it?
But we grow forgetful over time and only a handful of
years passed before Bad Prince Eugene was once again
known as a good prince.

And, unless you are very stupid, the rest you know
well. The cracked helmet, the shattered sword and the
jewelled gauntlets that Prince Eugene used in battle are
now displayed in a glass cabinet in the Schwartzgarten
Museum.

The Festival of Prince Eugene is held in the great city
every year to commemorate the defeat of Emeté Talbor.
And boys and girls are sent to their rooms with bags of
sugared noses, lest the spirit of Talbor should rise up and

slice off their own snouts with the tip of his sword. There is much merriment and laughter and once again I say 'Pah!' I have now lived to the age of seventy-five and, to my certain knowledge, have not laughed once these past sixty-five years. Laughter stunts the growth and addles the brain. It is of no use to man nor child.

Elka lived to a ripe age, and after a happy life came to rest in the Schwartzgarten Municipal Cemetery. Kalvitas makes chocolate in his shop to this very day, though he is more than ninety years of age. He still owns the sword he carried in battle and sometimes he will slice chocolates with it and tell of the heads he chopped off with the self-same blade.

And what of the name of the Seventh Founding Family, eh? The family that was unknowable?

I still do not know it.

So take your infernal questions and be gone with you.

EVER WATCHFUL

Don't miss a single
GRIZZLY sight in the city
of Schwartzgarten!

Turn the page for an extract
from the most trusted guide
to the great city…

MULLER·BRUN·&·GELLERHUND'S

SCHWARTZGARTEN
AN ILLUSTRATED GUIDE TO THE CITY AND ITS ENVIRONS

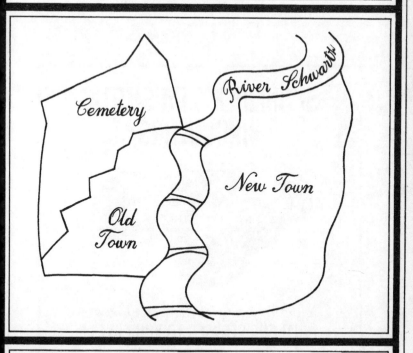

Cemetery

River Schwartz

New Town

Old Town

THE OLDEST AND MOST TRUSTED GUIDE TO THE GREAT CITY

"The traveller whose tankard is
drained in a single gulp
will be lost to the wolves by
nightfall."

*Traditional Schwartzgarten
Proverb*

A Pictorial and Descriptive Guide

TO
SCHWARTZGARTEN
&
THE NORTHERN REGIONS

INCLUDING

LAKE TANEVA, THE SUNKEN CITY
and the
BRAMMERHAUS ALPS

WITH STREET MAPS, MOTORING GUIDES AND
CAUTIONARY ADVICE TO ASSIST THE VISITOR
IN AVOIDING LOSS OF LIMB AND LIFE WHEN
TRAVERSING THESE PARTS

＊＊＊＊＊＊

Lavishly and Curiously Illustrated Throughout

＊＊＊＊＊＊

TWENTY-FIRST EDITION - REVISED

SCHWARTZGARTEN:

MULLER, BRUN & GELLERHUND
110 ALEXIS STREET, SCHWARTZGARTEN
AND AT THE SUNKEN CITY

WE RAISE OUR HATS
AND WELCOME YOU TO
SCHWARTZGARTEN

Unless visitors are fortunate enough to travel by scheduled Airship Service, most will arrive in Schwartzgarten by way of the *Imperial Railway Station* in the south of the Great City. The railway was erected on the instructions of Good Prince Eugene, who was himself a great patron of the railways and an enthusiast for all things mechanical. Worthy of note

The Twin Travellers welcoming passengers outside Schwartzgarten's Imperial Railway Station

are the statues of the *Twin Travellers* at the entrance to the station, their eyes shrouded by the hoods they wear – a reminder that all travellers stumble blindly in the darkness and none can ever be assured of their final destination.

The Emperor Xavier Hotel is but a short journey by taxicab from the railway station and offers superior accommodation for visitors of quality. Poorer travellers can seek room

The traditional Raven mask of the Vigils

and supper in the historic *Old Chop House* (once a haunt of Emeté Talbor's despised *Vigils*) or, in the Old Town, at any number of boarding houses (though cockroaches are plentiful and bedbugs more plentiful still).

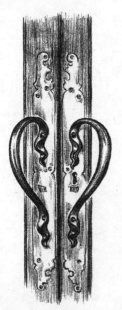

Door handles, Emperor Xavier Hotel

The Old Chop House

The tailors HEMPKELLER & BAUSCH and neighbouring premises occupy the site of the original settlement of Schwartzgarten, founded a thousand years and more ago by the Hungry Seven, as recorded in the Northern Manuscripts.

M. KALVITAS, the oldest surviving chocolate shop in Schwartzgarten, is still home to M. Kalvitas, the oldest surviving chocolate maker in the Great City.

Wherever the visitor chooses to stay, Schwartzgarten is a glittering jewel of the North and should be explored at leisure. Places of special interest include *Edvardplatz* at the very heart of the city with its notable clock tower, the excellent *Zoological Gardens*, the *Governor's Palace* with its celebrated Traitor's Gallery, and the vast sprawl of the *Schwartzgarten Municipal Cemetery*.

But for the earnest traveller who seeks a fuller knowledge of the dark ways and customs of our Great City, might we humbly recommend the *Schwartzgarten Museum* as the place to begin your journey? It is a veritable treasure trove of ghoulish mementoes and bloodthirsty relics cataloguing over a thousand years of tragedy, warfare and intrigue. If your heart has quickened at the very thought of such a place, then you are the visitor we seek and we bid you welcome.

So read on, dear traveller, and let Messers Muller, Brun & Gellerhund take you by the hand and guide you through the winding streets of Schwartzgarten.

But keep your wits sharp and your mind open, for who knows what strange delights and adventures the Great City holds in store for YOU?

The Gate of Skulls, entrance way to Schwartzgarten's Municipal Cemetery

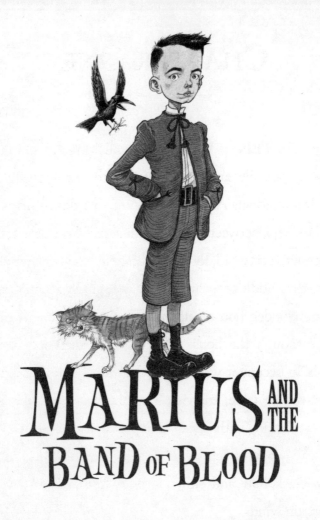

MARIUS AND THE BAND OF BLOOD

Read on for a sneak peek of the next instalment in the

TALES FROM SCHWARTZGARTEN

…if you dare.

CHAPTER ONE

❖

BLATTEN WAS a small town, clinging desperately and apologetically to the foothills of the Brammerhaus Alps. It was home to a dozen firms of weavers who, between them, manufactured the celebrated Brammerhaus tweed, for which Blatten was justly famous.

In the middle of the town, beside a spindly aspen, stood a large wooden house belonging to the Myerdorf family. Large though the house was, the only member of the family to occupy it was Marius Myerdorf, who sat alone at the dining table, enjoying a breakfast of cream cheese and rye bread, with sliced dill pickle and caperberries. He was a boy of ten, with dark, sorrowful eyes, short raven-black hair and skin pig-pink from the buffeting mountain winds.

There was a tentative knock at the dining room door and Marius's Tutor hurried into the room, clutching a letter tightly in his hand. He was a small man, barely taller and hardly ten years older than his student.

'I'm afraid I have some terrible news,' he gasped.

Marius dipped his pickle in the mound of cream cheese. 'Are my parents dead?' he asked.

This was not an unusual question for the boy to pose. Marius often felt quite certain that his parents had been the victims of unfortunate accidents. And in the past he had always been wrong. But even a stopped clock tells the correct time twice a day, and on this occasion Marius was perfectly justified in fearing the worst.

'Yes,' replied Mr Brunert, quietly. 'Your parents are dead.'

Marius looked up from his breakfast plate. 'You mean, really dead?'

The Tutor nodded gravely.

'How?' asked Marius.

'It was a cable car accident,' explained Mr Brunert. 'They had been skiing in the mountains, many hundreds of kilometres away from here.'

'They like skiing,' said Marius. He corrected himself. 'Liked skiing.' He stared hard at Mr Brunert and spoke in a whisper. 'Was it quick?'

Sadly, the Tutor shook his head.

'The cable car dropped many hundreds of metres into a

ravine, but it seems it was cushioned by a fresh fall of snow. Your parents may well have survived the drop, were it not for the presence of...' He halted, mid-sentence, uncertain how best to continue.

Fortunately, Marius broke the uncomfortable silence. 'The presence of wolves?'

'It would seem so,' replied Mr Brunert.

'Mother said that Father's fear of wolves was irrational,' said Marius, thoughtfully. 'I suppose she was wrong, wasn't she?'

'I suppose she was,' said the Tutor.

Marius had imagined so many times that an unfortunate accident had claimed the lives of his parents that it was difficult for him to absorb the fact that they were now indeed dead in their graves. Or rather, dead inside the bellies of a pack of ravening wolves.

The following morning the snow was falling heavily and Mr Brunert arranged by telephone to meet with Mr Offenhaus, Bank Manager to the Myerdorf family.

Mr Brunert had formed a peculiar aversion to the snow.

He shuddered at the prospect of stepping out through the front door and wrapped his striped woollen muffler tightly around his neck.

'We must be brave,' he said. 'Goodness knows how much money your parents have left you. I haven't been paid these last three months.'

Marius stared sadly at Mr Brunert; he was closer to a brother than a tutor, and the fact that the untimely and selfish death of his parents had further added to the man's woes troubled him greatly.

Forcing the door open against the howling wind, Mr Brunert guided Marius outside and together they set off for the banking house.

Mr Offenhaus was an old man, as fat as a bear with hair as white as a mountain weasel. He snuffled as he moved slowly around his office, crunching hard on a peppermint throat lozenge which perfumed the musty air. The pigeonholes on the wall behind him were stuffed full of aged vellum deeds and yellowing envelopes, and he leafed through the papers carefully, searching.

'Ah!' said Mr Offenhaus at last, and his arthritic fingers alighted claw-like on the files in question. 'Myerdorf.' He tugged out the necessary papers and laid them on his desk before easing himself slowly into his leather armchair.

Marius and Mr Brunert sat patiently, listening to the wind as it howled mournfully through the town before hammering against the window of the office and rattling the latch. At long last, Mr Offenhaus looked up from the papers and his gaze settled on Marius's tragic face.

'Dead, you say? Both your parents?'

Marius nodded. 'Wolves,' he said quietly.

Mr Offenhaus shook his head sympathetically. 'Fond of them, were you? Your mother and father?'

'I don't think they were very fond of me,' replied Marius.

'Serves them right, then,' said Mr Offenhaus, and his face ruptured into a broad grin. 'Wolves were too good for them, if you ask me.'

'Thank you,' said Marius politely. 'You're very kind.'

Mr Brunert attempted a gentle cough, which spluttered out of him like the beginnings of something tubercular. Mr Offenhaus shifted his gaze from boy to Tutor and proffered his box of peppermint lozenges.

'How much money did the Myerdorfs leave?' ventured Mr Brunert, sucking gratefully on a peppermint.

Mr Offenhaus frowned. 'But there is no money. Not a sorry curseling.'

'No money?' gasped Mr Brunert and choked quietly on his peppermint.

Mr Offenhaus shook his head. 'Unfortunately, Marius, your parents left you with a number of unpaid debts. The house must be sold, of course.'

'Then where will I live?' asked Marius.

'You have relatives, do you not?' replied the Bank Manager.

'I don't know,' said Marius. 'And even if I do, I don't want to live with them. Not if they're as bad as my parents. Can't Mr Brunert look after me for ever and for always?'

Mr Brunert turned and stared sadly out of the window. He had barely enough money to support himself, let alone a boy with a fondness for cocoa and cream cheese. When he finally spoke his voice trembled and the words caught in his throat as painfully as the peppermint lozenge.

'Have no fear, Marius,' he said. 'I will make sure that you will be taken in and cared for and will not be removed to the Schwartzgarten Reformatory for Maladjusted Children.'

Every night for a week Mr Brunert worked to compile a family tree for the Myerdorf family, sending telegrams first thing each morning in the hope of unearthing a kindly relative who would shower Marius with the love that his parents had always denied him. But it proved unaccountably difficult to trace surviving members of the Myerdorf family.

'Have you found anybody that actually wants me?' asked Marius gloomily one evening as Mr Brunert sat working by the light of a flickering candle.

'Come, Marius,' said his Tutor. 'It's not that your relatives don't wish to take you in. It's simply the fact that most of them are very unfortunately and inconveniently dead.'

It was hard for Marius not to take his family's high mortality rate personally. It seemed that they had selfishly chosen to die rather than offer him shelter.

But just when the boy was preparing to abandon all hope a telegram was delivered to the house, as Marius and Mr Brunert were preparing to sit down to a simple supper of cocoa and spiced mountain cheese.

'It would appear that you have a great-great uncle in Schwartzgarten,' said Mr Brunert, reading from the telegram. 'Did your parents ever speak of the man?'

Marius shook his head.

'How strange,' said Mr Brunert.

'My parents were very strange people,' replied Marius.

<hr/>

A week later a tiny white envelope arrived. It was addressed to Marius Myerdorf in an inky scrawl. The envelope contained a single rail ticket to Schwartzgarten, and an address, scrawled in the same elderly hand. There was nothing else. No card to greet the boy. No word of commiseration at the death of his parents. Nothing.

'I'm sure he's a very busy man,' said Mr Brunert, sensing Marius's disappointment. 'I have little doubt that he wished to despatch the railway ticket as quickly as possible and that there was not sufficient time for your aged relative to write an accompanying message.'

'How aged is he?' asked Marius.

'According to your family tree...' Mr Brunert stopped.

'Yes?' said Marius, impatiently.

'It appears that the benevolent gentleman is very nearly ninety years of age.'

'That's ancient,' said the boy with a frown. 'Do they keep him in a museum?'

'He may very well live for another couple of years… maybe even another five,' said the Tutor with an optimistic note in his voice that belied his true feelings on the matter.

'He'll probably be dead before I even arrive there,' said Marius. 'He would have been wise to send a return railway ticket instead.'

He picked up the ticket and turned it idly in his hands. Written on the back, in the same cramped hand as the address on the envelope, was a message so small it was barely visible to the naked eye. Marius strained his eyes and read:

Bring no inferior chocolate with you…

And beneath these words, written in blood-red ink, the message continued:

…on pain of death!

If you prefer CLEAVERS to kittens and FIENDS
to fairies...then you'll love the

GRUESOMELY FUNNY

TALES FROM
SCHWARTZGARTEN

ISBN 978 1 40831 455 5 pbk
ISBN 978 1 40831 668 9 eBook

ISBN 978 1 40831 456 2 pbk
ISBN 9781 40831 671 9 eBook

ISBN 9781 40833 181 1 hbk
ISBN 9781 40831 672 6 eBook

ISBN 9781 40833 182 8 hbk
ISBN 9781 40831 673 3 eBook